Hushed Up

A Myrtle Clover Cozy Mystery, Volume 15

Elizabeth Spann Craig

Published by Elizabeth Spann Craig, 2019.

HUSHED UP

First edition. November 19, 2019.

Written by Elizabeth Spann Craig.

For my family.

Chapter One

"It's no fun visiting someone who's asleep," said Myrtle in a reprimanding tone.

Her friend Miles immediately jerked his head up off his chest and looked abashed. "Sorry," he mumbled. "I haven't been sleeping well lately."

"Have you *ever* slept well, or is your insomnia a later-in-life thing?" asked Myrtle.

Miles sighed. "Believe it or not, there was a time when I slept like the dead. Now I'm on this bizarre sleep schedule. It could have something to do with people visiting me in the middle of the night," he said, giving Myrtle a sideways glance.

Myrtle frowned at him. "I only knock on your door when it's clear you're awake. If I see a light on, I know I'm not the only one who's up for the day at 3:30."

Miles said, "That's only part of it. *Everything* seems to be off. I eat breakfast at 4:00, then I'm hungry for lunch at 9:30 or 10:00. That puts supper at 3:00 in the afternoon. Before I know it, it's 7:30 in the evening and I'm nodding off over my book."

Myrtle said sternly, "That doesn't completely explain why you're falling asleep now. It's only 9:00 a.m."

Miles shrugged. "I guess the lack of sleep is catching up with me. And today isn't the day for that to happen."

"I still say you should simply have told the ladies no," said Myrtle, pursing her lips.

Miles held out his hands helplessly. "I was caught off-guard! I had no idea there was a plan afoot to invite me to join garden club."

"You keep your yard too tidy," said Myrtle. "They see you out there with your pair of clippers making sure all the blades of grass are exactly the same height."

"No, I really think it's because occasionally there's heavy lifting involved for garden club," said Miles thoughtfully.

Myrtle shrugged. "Then the husbands usually help out. And I drag Red into it."

Red was Myrtle's long-suffering son. He was never excited about helping out with Myrtle's garden club, but was always relieved she at least was keeping busy and out of trouble. And wasn't investigating murders.

Miles said, "Perhaps the husbands have revolted. After all, it couldn't be too pleasant to load and carry things for the botanical sale or the fundraising soiree. Maybe they just reached the point where they decided enough was enough."

"And they said 'no.' Which is exactly what you should have done, Miles!"

Miles said in a glum voice, "I've gotten very good at saying no via email. I've even gotten pretty good at saying it on a phone call. But when I'm approached at my front door, I'm apparently unable to do it."

Myrtle said, "You should simply have told them you needed time to consider it. That you have many other obligations and needed to see if you would be able to consistently make the meetings."

"They were holding balloons," said Miles forlornly. "It's hard to put anyone off when they seem so excited and they're holding a bunch of balloons."

Myrtle tilted her head thoughtfully. "Is that so? They must *really* need some help. It sounds like sorority rush. That's exactly what happened, Miles: you were rushed."

"Well, the pledge period seemed awfully short," said Miles. "Now I'm already in the stage of membership where they're making me do heavy-lifting."

"Or perhaps you're being hazed. What is it you're picking up today?"

Miles said, "I'm *supposed* to be picking up donations. That's actually the reason I'm here right now. Today is the last day for you to donate something for the garden club silent auction. Some people are giving away packages, some baskets of items, and some are donating individual things."

"What kinds of things are being donated?" Myrtle frowned and started a mental evaluation of her rather modest possessions.

Miles said, "Tippy is donating an 'experience package.'"

"What in heaven's name is that?"

"She has a travel agent friend who has helped her put together a trip to wine country with lodging and food," said Miles.

Myrtle scowled. "What are other people giving? *Regular* people?"

Miles said, "Is Blanche regular?"

"Perhaps more regular than Tippy is."

Miles said, "Blanche is donating a hot air balloon ride through a company in South Carolina."

Myrtle scowled. "Neither of those folks is regular, clearly." She sat deep in thought for a few moments and then snapped her fingers. "I know. I have something that might be of some interest for a certain type of person."

She walked into the back of her house and returned with a small, framed sketch. "Will this do?"

Miles pushed his glasses up his nose and studied the artwork. He nodded. "I think this will do the trick. So, this is an artist's rendition of downtown Bradley? Circa . . . ?"

Myrtle said, "From about fifty years ago. He was actually drawing what he saw, not drawing from memory. It's kind of fun to see what stores were around then."

"You took this off your wall, though. You won't miss it?"

"Oh, no. I remember very easily what downtown Bradley looked like fifty years ago. I wasn't even particularly young," said Myrtle with a snort. "Besides, having this off my mind is a relief. I was fretting over the stupid donation since Tippy announced the blasted silent auction."

Miles nodded. "I know what you mean. Fortunately, they didn't make me participate since I'm such a new member."

Myrtle raised her eyebrows. "Then you *are* still in the pledge period, after all." She glanced at the clock. "After you make your rounds, do you want to come back by? I have some of the best-looking tomatoes you've ever seen. I can make us tomato sandwiches and we can watch *Tomorrow's Promise*."

Miles said, "As long as the show is particularly riveting. I need to stay awake, remember?"

"It's a soap opera. Being riveting is its stock-in-trade."

Miles nodded and stood up, stretching a little. "All right. I'm off to Lillian Johnson's house, then."

"Now *she's* something of a regular person! What are you picking up there?" asked Myrtle.

"It's a basket called 'Dog Days.' It's going to be heavy," Miles added gloomily.

"What's in it?"

"A dog bed, a feeding station, toys, treats, grooming set, the works," said Miles.

"Does Lillian even *own* a dog?" Myrtle frowned.

"I hope not. Lillian said she'd leave the door unlocked for me in case she's not home. All I need is an overprotective pet assuming I'm some sort of threat to its property." Miles shuddered.

"For your sake, I hope Lillian *isn't* there. She's nothing but trouble."

Miles raised his eyebrows. "Well, that's not the kind of statement you can just throw out there without any explanation."

Myrtle waved her hand around impatiently. "She gossips, for one."

"Isn't that what we're doing now?" asked Miles.

"Yes, but she does it *maliciously*. Lillian is quite malicious," said Myrtle with a bite in her tone.

"How awful," said Miles dryly.

"It isn't only that, either. She hangs out with Erma Sherman. That should tell you something about her," said Myrtle with a sniff.

Erma Sherman was Myrtle's next-door neighbor. Myrtle considered Erma to be her nemesis.

Miles said, "Everyone needs a friend, don't they?"

"That's debatable when the subject is Erma. Anyway, they seem to have lots in common. That's a bad sign right there. Plus, there's the fact Wanda warned me about her."

Miles leaned forward slightly. "Really? What did Wanda say?"

Myrtle shifted uncomfortably. "That's not the point. The point is, Wanda mentioned her."

"But in what *capacity*?" pushed Miles.

"What does it matter? You never believe Wanda has a gift at all," said Myrtle.

Miles said slowly, "But the fact of the matter is, Wanda seems to know things. I don't know how she does, but she does. And if Lillian is dangerous in any way, I think I have a right to know that before I head over to her house to pick up a silent auction donation."

Myrtle looked cross. "All right, then. Wanda's prediction wasn't to stay away from Lillian. It was that Lillian was in danger."

Miles relaxed a bit. "Well, but that's Wanda's stock prediction, isn't it? She always thinks people are in danger."

"Because they are," said Myrtle, still irritated. "Anyway, when I attempted to share Wanda's warning with Lillian, she was not receptive."

Miles snorted. "I can only imagine."

"She should have been appreciative that Wanda was looking after her! And that I had passed along the message. People are so ungrateful these days," said Myrtle with a sniff.

"What did Lillian say?"

"She acted as if I were completely senile. Lillian acted so condescending. Then she asked Erma Sherman to keep an eye on me. And she threatened to tell Red about the whole thing." Now Myrtle was in danger of sulking. The thought of Red brought it out in her.

Miles looked uncomfortable, as he frequently did when he and Myrtle were discussing Wanda. "Maybe Wanda meant something different."

Myrtle frowned at him. "How could you possibly mean something different when you tell someone they're in danger? *Lillian, you're in danger of spending too much money on a silent auction basket?*"

Miles shrugged. "I'm only saying maybe she didn't mean an outcome as dire as she usually does."

"*Lillian, you're in danger of getting cavities if you don't go in for a cleaning?*" Myrtle shook her head. "Wanda doesn't deal in the trivial."

"Of course she does! Think about her horoscopes for the paper. You know as well as I do that half of them have to do with Wanda warning someone they need to take their dog to the vet or their roses will be eaten by Japanese beetles unless they spray them."

Myrtle said impatiently, "So her gift is a broad one. She can advise on big problems and small ones. But when she says someone is in danger, they're in danger. And if Lillian read the paper, she'd know Wanda wasn't a quack and neither am I."

Miles walked toward the door. "Well, at least perhaps I can relieve your mind. I'm heading over there first and I'll report in. Even if she's not there, there should be breakfast dishes still in the sink or other signs of life."

"*My* mind doesn't have to be relieved. I wrote off Lillian Johnson as soon as she started looking at me as if I were crazy."

Miles said, "I can relieve Wanda's then. I know she worries about people."

Myrtle's expression softened a little. "That's true. All right, just let me know."

But when Miles called just fifteen minutes later, he said grimly, "Myrtle, Lillian is dead."

Chapter Two

The problem, thought Myrtle as she held herself stiffly in Erma Sherman's car, was that Lillian lived too far away. She'd never thought that was a problem before, but now, heading out to join Miles, it was clear it was a problem of great import. She'd had to knock on Erma's door since Red's wife, Elaine, wasn't home and Myrtle no longer owned a car.

The only good thing was Erma was unnaturally solemn and rather quiet as she drove her large boat of a car to Lillian's house.

Myrtle reveled in the silence until Erma broke it, looking sideways at her. "Did Miles say what happened to Lillian?"

Myrtle shook her head. "No. He only said she was dead. He needed to call Red and let him know."

Red would likely not look kindly on Myrtle's presence there, but he would have to understand she needed to support Miles. And, naturally, find out exactly what was going on.

"Well, Lillian and I used to talk about her health problems. Did you know she and I had some of the same ones? Our stomachs and intestines were never right. I told her she should go see my gastro doctor. Did she listen, though? She never did! Because my insides always felt all twisted up inside until I started seeing Dr. Talveston."

Myrtle hurriedly cut in. One of Erma's favorite topics of conversation was her bowels and Myrtle did not have the stomach for it, today of all days. "I'm fairly certain Lillian's sudden death wasn't a result of her intestines." Not, anyway, if Miles had been in such a rush to get off the phone with her to call Red.

Finally, Erma pulled up in front of Lillian's house, which was already cordoned off with police tape. Miles appeared to be perched in the back of Red's police car and looking rather pale. Myrtle saw Red spin around and roll his eyes when he saw his mother. He strode over to Erma's car and hissed, "Mama, what are you doing here?"

Myrtle smiled complacently at him. "I'm here to help Miles, of course. It isn't every day he comes face-to-face with tragedy."

"You can help him a lot more if you meet him over at Bo's Diner in about twenty minutes. I'm sure he'll be ready to eat by then and he likely can use a little distraction. Plus, he seems completely exhausted."

"He hasn't slept for a while," said Myrtle with a shrug.

"Oh, and give him a bottle of hand-sanitizer. He keeps wiping his hands on his trousers and saying he forgot his," said Red.

Erma clambered out of her car and hurried around the hood to stand with Red. Red's expression indicated he was not exactly pleased to see Erma there, either.

"Hi, Red," trilled Erma. "It's a terrible tragedy, isn't it?" But Erma couldn't seem to wipe an excited smile off her face. "You know Lillian and I were friends. We saw each other *all* the time.

So feel free to ask me any questions because I can answer them. You have a notebook, don't you?"

Myrtle could always tell when Red was getting annoyed. That might be because it happened so often in her presence. A red flush rose from his neck. She suspected Red had high blood pressure, although he always brushed her off when she asked. Of course, he was always nosy about *her* medical visits, even though he never talked about his own. Which was completely unfair.

She had to hand it to him, though; he answered Erma very politely, although he seemed to be speaking through clenched teeth. "Do you know anything that's directly related to Lillian's death?"

Erma considered this. "Well, she had this terrible bout with her bowels. I always say you can tell a lot about a person's overall health by their bowels."

Red quickly interjected before Erma could go into excruciating detail, "Erma, Lillian's death wasn't a natural one. I'm afraid the state of her bowels had nothing to do with it."

This made Erma gawk at him, open-mouthed. "Not natural? You mean, *murder*?" She now looked even more excited.

Red nodded, looking toward the road as if hoping for the cavalry to appear. Or, possibly, the state police. "When was the last time you spoke with Lillian?"

Erma hesitated and then became flustered. "Well, you see, we were such good friends that we didn't have to speak to each other every day. We were simpatico, you know. We always picked right up where we left off."

Myrtle rolled her eyes.

Erma pinched her face up in an effort to think. "Tuesday. I think we spoke on Tuesday. Yes! Actually, that's exactly when we spoke. Because Lillian was upset about *her*!" She swung around, arm outstretched and pointed squarely at Myrtle.

Myrtle glared at Erma.

Red rubbed his face and spoke through his hands. "Mama, why was Lillian mad at you?"

"Does it even matter? I wasn't mad at *her*, if that's what you're getting at. I had nothing to do with Lillian's death. I simply thought her very, very silly," said Myrtle with irritation.

Miles was watching with interest from the police car. Apparently, he started feeling steadier on his feet and slightly more awake because he stood and started in their direction.

Erma was getting even more keyed up. She raised her hand as if she were waiting to be called on in school. "I know! I know why she was mad at Myrtle. It was because of that psychic."

Red closed his eyes. "Wanda?"

"That's it! Wanda," said Erma, pleased with herself for contributing something important. "Don't you need to write that down in your notebook?"

Red ignored this, staring at his mother instead. "Please tell me Wanda isn't involved in this."

"Of *course* she's not," said Myrtle crossly as Miles joined them. "She was simply trying to be helpful. Which was a colossal waste of her time considering how Lillian received the information."

Red said, "So Wanda spoke to Lillian?"

"Absolutely not! Wanda doesn't make house calls. No, she relayed the information to me and I provided it to Lillian. And Lillian was heedless. Recklessly so." Myrtle sniffed.

"What was this information?"

Myrtle said, "That she was in danger. And here she is, dead. Clearly, yet another accurate prediction from Wanda."

Red absently reached up a hand to rub the side of his forehead as if it were throbbing.

"Why did Wanda think she was in danger? Did Wanda know Lillian?"

Myrtle snorted. "Wanda? Know a florist? No. She used her gifts, Red. And you know that's not how The Sight works. Wanda didn't have a *reason* for Lillian to be in danger. She simply knew she was."

"That's not how The Sight works," mumbled Red, shaking his head. "I can't believe I'm going to have to include Wanda in my report on this case. So Mama, you visited Lillian on Tuesday?"

"That's right. I felt it was my duty to inform her," said Myrtle primly.

"And she wasn't receptive to this information?"

Miles hid a smile.

"Lillian was completely pigheaded about it! She showed me the door. Didn't even offer me a glass of water and it was a *very* hot day," said Myrtle indignantly.

Red raised his eyebrows. "So, at any rate, we know *you* were unhappy with Lillian Johnson."

"As I said, I had nothing to do with her death," said Myrtle sullenly.

Red looked up at the sound of cars approaching. "Looks like the state police are here. I'm going to need to talk to them briefly. Y'all are all excused." He looked at Miles. "I was telling Mama earlier that you looked like you should head over to Bo's Diner and get something to eat. You look a little peaked. You could meet Mama and Erma there."

"You must be getting a commission for sending people over there," grumbled Myrtle. The last thing she wanted was to spend lunch with Erma. But now she knew Lillian was murdered, it could be there was some actual information she might be able to provide. As difficult as that was to believe.

Miles said, "That might be a good idea. I didn't have much breakfast. Myrtle, do you have any hand sanitizer I could borrow?"

Myrtle fished a bottle out of her huge purse and Miles looked much-relieved as he slathered some on his hands.

"I don't think murder is catching, Miles," said Myrtle with irritation. Then she suddenly stopped short, staring across the yard at a tall man with a short, military-style haircut who was unfolding himself from a police car. "It's Lieutenant Perkins!"

Myrtle walked toward him. Miles said, "Myrtle, I think we were dismissed."

"That was before I saw my old friend had arrived. I'm sure he'll want to catch up."

Miles looked more doubtful as he followed Myrtle at a distance. Erma had spotted a neighbor watching the proceedings with concern and was excitedly updating her while somehow making herself the star of the story at the same time.

Red spotted his mother's determined approach and held up a hand. "Mama, we're on official police business."

"I know that," she answered crisply. "Why else would Lt. Perkins be here? I merely want to say hello, that's all."

Red watched suspiciously as Myrtle greeted Lt. Perkins.

"It's so good to see you again, Mrs. Clover," said Perkins courteously. He looked as cool and unruffled as usual and, to Myrtle's mind, was in stark contrast to Red, who was getting decidedly flushed and bent out of shape.

"Well, I know it was good to say hi, Mama, but I need to speak with the lieutenant," said Red quickly.

"Not before I invite him over to have a meal with me," said Myrtle sweetly. "I've asked him before but things have been so crazy that we've only been able to meet at the diner. This time, I'd like to cook him a *real* meal."

Red and Miles exchanged looks. Myrtle's cooking was legendary, and not in a good way.

Red said, "And once again, Lt. Perkins finds himself very, very busy, Mama."

Perkins smiled at Myrtle and for once his eyes actually crinkled up at the corners. "You know, I think I *would* enjoy a real, home-cooked meal."

Myrtle beamed at him. "Well, I'm just as pleased as punch! Would you like to come over tonight? I'm sure I could whip something up."

Red gave Perkins a meaningful look and said, "Actually, I think we're still going to be hashing through this case tonight. Maybe tomorrow morning would be better, before he kicks off the day."

Myrtle gave her son an annoyed look. "You understand this is a *private* breakfast, Red. It's just me and Lt. Perkins. And maybe Miles," she said, including her sidekick in a half-hearted manner.

Red looked up at the heavens as if seeking patience there. "That's absolutely fine. I certainly don't want to crash your breakfast party. I understand you're only being difficult because I was upset at the revolt you led at Greener Pastures retirement home."

A smile pulled at the lieutenant's lips and Miles dissolved into one of his odd coughing fits again.

"You shouldn't be so angry, Red. You know it does things to your blood pressure. Besides, it wasn't a revolt at all. It was a perfectly peaceful march to the management. The only way a revolt figured into the equation at all was the food. *It* was revolting. They've changed their food vendor to save money and the poor inmates—"

"*Residents*," said Red.

"The poor inmates have been eating like children every day. Who gives chicken tenders and fish sticks to octogenarians? Cheese dippers with marinara sauce? What kind of statement were they trying to make? The menu is condescending, I tell you," said Myrtle.

Perkins said thoughtfully, "I think I did hear about some sort of uprising at the retirement home lately."

Myrtle looked pleased. Sensing a more sympathetic audience she said, "The food is frequently served cold and that place is way too expensive for folks to have to eat cold fish sticks. The vegetables are weird, too."

"Weird vegetables?" asked Miles, pushing his glasses farther up his nose.

"Yes. Beets. Beets, I tell you! What happened to good, old-fashioned broccoli or spinach? What's wrong with those people?"

Red rolled his eyes. "Now, thanks to you, the residents' rates will go up and they'll switch food vendors. Problem solved."

Perkins said smoothly, "Breakfast sounds lovely, Mrs. Clover. Is early all right?"

Myrtle gave him a big smile, "I frequently get up for the day at three a.m. Any time after that is fine."

Perkins said, "Let's make it seven-thirty."

Red murmured, "And breakfast, fortunately, is a difficult meal to mess up."

Chapter Three

A few minutes later, Miles got into his car and Myrtle climbed reluctantly back into Erma's. She hadn't been quick enough to think of a good excuse to ride there with Miles.

It was the ride over to the diner that was most annoying to Myrtle.

Erma said with a sidelong glance, "You don't think Wanda did this, do you? I'm just asking because you always do that detecting work."

Myrtle swung around to glare at Erma. "What on earth are you implying?" she asked coldly.

Erma kept on going, not even registering Myrtle's displeasure. "Wanda knew something."

"Of *course* she knew something. She is psychic." Myrtle glared at Erma.

"Wanda knew Lillian was going to die," persisted Erma.

"Wanda knew Lillian was in *danger* and felt a responsibility to warn her of that. Because she didn't think she'd be taken seriously, Wanda asked me to relay the information. If Lillian was too foolhardy to pay attention, that's completely her own fault and absolutely nothing to do with Wanda."

Erma was still apparently mulling things over. Considering Erma's intelligence level, it was a sluggish and painful process. "Was Miles dating Lillian? Is that why he was at her house?"

"Certainly not! Miles is a new member of the garden club and was simply picking up Lillian's donation for the silent auction. Erma, you need to stop trying to connect the dots. The conclusions you're drawing are wildly inaccurate."

Myrtle was relieved they'd finally made it to downtown Bradley and the diner. Erma found a parking place in the front and Miles pulled in right next to them. Thankfully, the usually-crowded diner seemed to be having a slow day. They were able to get a table immediately.

Myrtle was determined this lunch with Erma would be as quick as possible. She didn't even look at the menu. "I know what I want. A pimento cheese dog with chili fries. Miles, you usually get the salad."

Miles, for some reason, was studying the menu as if he'd never eaten at Bo's Diner before. "I've never tried their fried chicken."

Erma said, "Oh, it's *wonderful*. The breading is yummy. And it comes with these buttery green beans. I've found them very easy to digest."

Myrtle gave Miles her best retired-teacher-stare. They needed to avoid talk of Erma's digestive activities at all cost during lunch. "The fried chicken might take a while to prepare."

Erma gave her braying laugh. "No way! They have a fryer ready to go. It'll just take minutes."

Myrtle said, "Do you know what you want, Erma?"

Now Erma, who had been very confident about what Miles should order, suddenly looked unsure. "This is tough. I either want the meat-and-three vegetable platter or the country fried steak and gravy."

Myrtle said briskly, "That's easy. Pick one and have the other the next time you come."

"But I don't go out very often."

Miles started coughing behind his laminated menu. His cough, to Myrtle's ears, sounded suspiciously like a laugh.

"Then order one for take-out and eat it for supper! Really, Erma, this is not brain surgery," said Myrtle crossly.

But Erma continued debating the pros and cons of the two dishes until the waitress came by a second time.

Myrtle said between gritted teeth, "Erma, I have things to do at home."

Erma, who'd been chewing her nails as she'd fretted over the monumental decision, said, "Okay. I'll get the meat-and-three."

The waitress asked, "Great. Which meat and which three vegetables?"

This spawned another few minutes of agony as Erma attempted to pick them from a fairly robust list on the menu.

Finally, the ordeal was over and the waitress trotted off to place their order. Myrtle opened her mouth to quickly broach the subject of Lillian's murder, but Erma beat her to it.

"Okay, so if Wanda wasn't involved in killing Lillian, then who was?" Erma leaned forward over the Formica table to stare at Myrtle and Miles.

"Shouldn't you be telling us? You were Lillian's friend, after all. What were her relationships like?" asked Myrtle. "The people closest to her are usually the most-likely suspects. Who would those people be?"

Erma's rodent-like features pursed in thought. "Lillian and her daughter, Annie, didn't get along. Lillian was *so* generous to her and offered her a job. Annie wouldn't even take it. Guess she thought she was too good for it or something. That's what Lillian thought, anyway."

Miles asked, "What did Lillian do?"

Myrtle said, "She was a florist. Had her own shop downtown. But not everyone is cut out to be a florist. Did Lillian *want* Annie to be a florist?"

Erma shrugged. "She said Annie wanted to leave town and find her fortune."

Miles frowned. "That's an odd turn of phrase for someone in her twenties."

Erma said, "Maybe she said something different, but the gist was the same. And then there's that woman who works for her. She saw her every day."

"Why would an employee kill her employer?"

"You said people close to her. If she saw the woman every day, she was pretty close to her."

"Was there anyone else?" asked Myrtle.

"Lillian and that caterer guy weren't getting along," said Erma, still screwing up her face in thought.

"What caterer guy is that? You mean Rowan Blain? The one who's catering the silent auction for the garden club?"

At the mention of the silent auction, Miles shifted uncomfortably as if his stomach hurt.

"Yeah. Rowan and Lillian didn't get along," said Erma. "Guess they saw each other too much at weddings and such since he was catering food and she was doing flowers."

Myrtle asked, "Didn't Lillian have a son, too?"

"Martin." Erma brightened. "He's a nice guy. Always joking and laughing. Lillian liked him a lot."

"But she didn't try to make *him* be a florist?"

"Nope. She'd pegged Annie for that. Martin had other plans—big plans, not flower shop plans. He's got lots of money and drives a nice car," said Erma. "He lives on the lake and has big parties out there."

"And what does he *do*?" asked Myrtle.

Erma was vague on this. "He's an entrepreneur."

"Hm," said Myrtle. Myrtle had opinions about people who called themselves entrepreneurs. So often they weren't exactly what they made themselves out to be.

The food arrived and Erma delved into her veggies with gusto. Myrtle figured, with any luck, she would be done in mere minutes. Of course, Miles was nibbling at his food like a rabbit, which would only drag the meal out longer. But maybe Myrtle could give him a kick under the table and talk about the virtues of to-go boxes and finishing one's food later.

Erma said something, which was completely unintelligible around her mouthful of food. She started coughing and then choking while Miles gazed at her with wide-eyed alarm.

"For heaven's sake, Erma, drink some water! Don't try to talk," snapped Myrtle.

She was vastly relieved when Erma regained control and Myrtle wasn't needed to perform a Heimlich maneuver.

Erma gasped for breath for a few moments, face flushed, before giving a sheepish grin.

Miles said politely, "You were saying, Erma?"

Myrtle gave him a look to indicate he shouldn't encourage her.

Erma said, "I was just saying that when I was talking to the next-door neighbor, she was kind of interesting. Do you remember when I was talking to her?" She peered at Myrtle.

"Of course I remember! It was only forty-five minutes ago," said Myrtle irritably. It was very annoying when people treated her as if her memory was shot to pieces.

"Well, I didn't know her, but I got to meet her. I was explaining Lillian and I were very close friends. Did you know Lillian and I used to do things together all the time? Sometimes we'd go for lunch. Sometimes we go out for dinner. Sometimes we just sat around and talked about health stuff."

Myrtle said between gritted teeth, "Just the headlines, Erma. Who was this neighbor?"

Erma seemed to be experiencing memory issues of her own, however. "Let's see. She had a weird name. I mean, it was a pretty name, but it wasn't a name like *Jane* or *Amy* or something like that. I think it started with a 't.'"

"Tonya?" asked Miles helpfully.

"Tina? Tori? Tammy? Teresia? Terri? Trish?" asked Myrtle, tossing out names haphazardly in her effort to wrap this lunch up for good.

"Noooooo," said Erma slowly. She screwed her face up tightly again to remember. Then she snapped her fingers. "Got it!

Tallulah. So I was telling Tallulah about all the things Lillian and I would do together and how close we were."

Myrtle attempted to get the conversation back on track. "Erma, I'm guessing there's a point to this. Something to do with the *interesting thing* Tallulah said?"

"Right. Anyway, when I was telling her about Lillian and me, she broke in and interrupted. She was really being kind of rude," said Erma thoughtfully, as if the realization just struck her. "She said she didn't understand how I could have spent so much time with Lillian when Lillian was such a difficult person to be around."

Miles lifted an eyebrow and Myrtle said, "Did Tallulah say what made Lillian difficult?"

"Nope." Erma shrugged. "That was it. I just thought it was sort of weird when I was saying such nice things about Lillian. And the fact Lillian had just died and everything. A neighbor should have been more upset about it." Her eyes widened. "Maybe *she* killed Lillian! And I was just talking to her."

Myrtle said, "It's a long way from thinking someone is difficult to killing them." She looked at her watch and gave Miles a very pointed look. "I think it's time for me to leave. I have some very important things to do."

Miles looked down at his half-eaten meal.

"I will get you a to-go box," said Myrtle briskly.

Erma gave them a jolly wave as she drove away from Bo's Diner. Myrtle gave a sigh of relief. "Thank heavens that's over. Now onto other things."

Miles asked hopefully, "Like going to your house and watching *Tomorrow's Promise* while I finish my lunch?"

"No, I think our plans have been completely derailed. I need to talk to Sloan Jones about the story I'm writing on Lillian's demise," said Myrtle, heading in the direction of the newspaper office that was just a few doors down. Sloan Jones was the editor of the paper and Myrtle was a correspondent.

Miles said, "If it's all the same to you, Myrtle, I think I'll skip that visit. I know exactly how it's going to go: he's going to say Red doesn't want you to write crime stories. He'll remind you that your helpful hints column is due. Then you'll argue you'll have a better perspective on the story than anyone else. Begrudgingly, Sloan will allow you to work on the article. I'll just sit in my car and wait for you with the air conditioning running and eat the rest of my lunch."

"That's fine. And I think you're wrong, Miles. Sloan knows by now that I *always* end up getting my way. He may just skip the whole arguing part. But suit yourself."

A moment later, she pushed open the wooden doors of the newspaper office. She let her eyes adjust to the dim interior and her nose adjust to the musty smell of old papers. Sloan was a former student of Myrtle's and his traditional response to her sudden appearances was to leap to attention and start falling all over himself as if he were late with his homework again.

This time, though, Sloan barely noticed she'd walked in the doors. She sat down next to him and he finally obligingly turned his office chair toward her, the wheels groaning in protest at his considerable weight shifting. "Hi there, Miss Myrtle."

"Everything going all right, Sloan?" asked Myrtle sharply. "You seem a little off."

Sloan heaved a sigh. "Is it that obvious?"

Myrtle said, "Very. It isn't Sally again, is it? This on-again, off-again nonsense really can't be healthy for your mental well-being."

Sloan shook his head. "Oh, no. No, it's finally all over with Sally and I couldn't be happier. It's like a huge weight has been lifted off my shoulders. No, this is about Katrina."

Myrtle frowned. "I don't know any Katrinas."

"She's fairly new to town. I've seen her a few times when I've gone out after work." He had a silly, mooning expression on his face.

Myrtle said briskly, "And you have a lot in common? Similar interests? You get along well?"

Sloan gave her a horrified look. "Miss Myrtle, I haven't even said hello to her yet."

"You mean you're just worshipping her from afar? Sloan, that's no way to start a relationship. You need to be friendly. Introduce yourself."

Sloan shook his head. "Not yet. I've got to move really slowly."

"Well, maybe you need to at least move to a closer barstool when you see her. And I probably wouldn't stare too much." Myrtle paused. "Sloan, this may come as a surprise to you, but I actually didn't come to the newspaper to discuss your love life."

Sloan said, "Hmm?"

Myrtle said, "Focus, Sloan. Look, I need to write that story on Lillian Johnson and I have just the angle to do it."

Sloan now seemed to be paying a little more attention. In fact, he appeared confused. "A story on Lillian Johnson? What, like a retrospective on her career as a florist?"

Myrtle gave him a severe look. "No, like an article reporting her violent death."

Sloan's eyebrows flew up on his large forehead. "What? When did that happen?"

"This morning. And it's rather alarming the newspaper editor doesn't know about it," said Myrtle crisply. "Really, Sloan, you need to pull yourself together."

It was her old schoolteacher tone and it seemed to finally snap Sloan into shape. He flushed and sat up a bit straighter in his chair. "So, she was murdered?"

"She was murdered and Miles found her. And Wanda predicted she was in danger before Lillian's death," said Myrtle.

Sloan's eyebrows bounced up his forehead again. "That will be an interesting angle. Wanda is very, very popular with our readers for her horoscopes, but it will be good to pull her into an article. I think the readers would really go for that."

"I'll have to get her permission, of course," said Myrtle offhandedly.

"Will you?" asked Sloan. "She's an employee of the paper, after all. And her name is already in the paper every single week. It's not like she's anonymous or anything."

"Still, I think it's important," said Myrtle firmly. She glanced over at Sloan's desk which was, as usual, a riot of papers and photographs and reference books. Since Sloan's unfortunate love life had been such a distraction lately, the paper had taken something of a backseat. Some days, the newspaper was barely printing by the deadline. Other days, Myrtle had to correct most of the stories because of Sloan's lax editing. "How is everything going with the paper?" she asked pointedly.

"Oh, it's going all right." Sloan shrugged. He gave Myrtle a sidelong glance. "Having a few issues with Elaine, though."

Myrtle winced. Red's wife was a wonderful woman and interested in a variety of hobbies. Sadly, she never seemed to have much talent for any of them, although that never dampened her enthusiasm. "What now?" she asked.

"Well, she's still doing social media postings for the paper and those have been pretty good," said Sloan quickly as if determined to say something positive first.

"Fewer pictures of her thumbs?" asked Myrtle.

"That's right. She seems to be aware she *has* thumbs now and that they are fond of getting in the way of the subjects, which is a good thing."

Myrtle said, "So what's the problem?"

Sloan sighed. "Elaine has a new hobby."

"Uh-oh," said Myrtle. "Although I can't say I'm surprised. It was about time for one to crop up. What is it this time? Calligraphy? Fishing? Organic gardening?"

"Writing," said Sloan.

Myrtle frowned. "You mean she wants to be a journalist?"

Sloan looked sad. "No. No, that might be easier to deal with. She's writing poetry and short stories. Elaine asked me whether I thought the paper could use a 'literary corner' once a week. That she'd be happy to get things rolling with some of her own work."

"And did you see this work?" asked Myrtle.

"I'm afraid so."

Myrtle said slowly, "I see." She followed that briskly with, "Well, that should be easy enough to deal with. You simply have to tell her the paper doesn't have enough room for any new columns. Or there's no demand for it. Or your advertisers wouldn't think literature was a good fit for the readership. And it isn't! The readers are hooked on Wanda's horoscopes, for heaven's sake. They wouldn't know what to do with poetry."

Sloan said glumly, "I know. That's what I need to do. And I will . . . it's just that she was so earnest."

"And she can stay earnest—she just needs to keep her stories and poetry unpublished, that's all. Okay, I'll shoot that story over later this afternoon, all right? Make sure to reserve room on the front page."

She hoped Sloan was paying attention. He now appeared to be looking at pictures of his crush on social media.

Chapter Four

When Myrtle returned to the car, Miles was fast asleep and snoring lightly, his empty take-out container on the passenger seat. He didn't even wake up when Myrtle took the container and threw it away in a nearby trash can. He didn't wake up when Myrtle slammed the passenger door after plopping down heavily into the car. So Myrtle opened and shut the door again with even more vigor until he finally stirred.

"Thank heavens," Myrtle said, "I was starting to believe I was sitting next to a corpse."

Miles blinked a few times and then rubbed his eyes. "Sorry. I'm just really tired from all that lost sleep."

Myrtle gave him a critical look as he continued rubbing the sleep from his eyes. "I'll drive, instead. You're way too sleepy to be alert enough to safely get us where we need to go."

This seemed to wake Miles up. "No, no. I can drive." He paused. "Where *do* we need to go? Wasn't the plan to go back to your house? I thought we were going to watch the soap opera."

Myrtle frowned. "You're certainly stuck on the soap opera today."

Miles sighed. "I wish you'd never gotten me hooked on them. The way they close each episode with a cliffhanger is very sneaky. I want to find out if Payton and Miranda were able to slip out of the government lab before the security guards rushed in."

"You know Payton and Miranda somehow got out of it. It wouldn't be much of a soap opera if the two of them ended up in jail for years," said Myrtle.

"Yes, but I want to know *how* they got out," persisted Miles.

Myrtle said, "And I do, too. But let's do that after we visit Wanda."

Miles looked uncomfortable, as he always did when the psychic was mentioned. He'd discovered he was a cousin of hers and felt a sense of responsibility for her, especially since she always seemed so downtrodden.

"Let me run by the ATM first," he said with a sigh.

They were about halfway there when Miles's phone rang and he startled. Myrtle barked, "Eyes on the road! I'll answer it."

Miles asked, "Can you see who it is?"

Myrtle peered at his phone. "It's Tippy Chambers."

Miles clutched the steering wheel with white-knuckled hands. "Oh, no. She's going to ask how the silent auction collection went. And it was totally derailed."

Myrtle quirked an eyebrow at him. "What's the worst that can happen? You get kicked out of garden club? That sounds like a positive outcome as far as I can tell." She answered the phone. "Tippy? It's Myrtle. Miles is driving."

"Oh, hi, Myrtle. Listen, I was just checking in to see if Miles was able to pick up the items for the auction. I thought he was going to drop them by my house." Tippy's cultured voice was a little strained. Myrtle remembered she tended to get a little keyed up before events.

Miles hazarded a stressed look at Myrtle and Myrtle gestured pointedly at the road. "Tippy, the truth is that Miles set out early today to start collecting auction items and then ran into something quite tragic. He found Lillian Johnson dead in her home."

There was silence on the other end. "Tippy?" prompted Myrtle.

"I'm so sorry to hear that," said Tippy. "How absolutely horrible. Was her death . . . I mean, did she suffer some sort of health calamity?" Her voice indicated she certainly hoped so.

"I'm afraid not. Lillian was murdered," said Myrtle.

Tippy paused again and then said slowly, "I see. Oh, goodness."

"Clearly, he didn't pick up Lillian's donation. And, afterward, he didn't just feel as if he could continue on picking up donations as if nothing had happened."

Miles nodded fervently.

Tippy said, "Of course not. How awful. This does change things quite a bit. I'm not sure how it would appear to the community if we just blithely continued on with the silent auction as if nothing had transpired. Wouldn't that seem very insensitive? Lillian was an important member of our club. And what would her family think?"

These questions didn't seem to be rhetorical, so Myrtle answered them. "I'm planning on bringing a sympathy casserole to Lillian's son and daughter tomorrow. I'll ask them personally what they think the garden club should do about the silent auction."

Miles gave her another sidelong look at the mention of the casseroles and Myrtle gestured impatiently at the road.

Tippy said with relief, "Would you? That would be wonderful, Myrtle. And tell Miles to just put the rest of the auction collecting on hold until you check in with the family. I'll send an email out to the club to let them know what's going on."

Myrtle hung up the phone and said, "Well, you're temporarily off the hook for collecting the rest of the stuff for the auction."

Miles said guiltily, "I'd actually completely forgotten about it once I saw Lillian. It was as if garden club ceased to exist. It might also have to do with my total lack of sleep. Besides, I can't even get Lillian's things. I'm sure they're in labeled bags and locked up at the police station."

Myrtle frowned. "Why on earth would her dog basket items be at the police station?"

Miles said, "Because the dog feeding station was the murder weapon."

"*What?*"

"Whoever killed Lillian picked up that heavy dog feeding station and whacked her over the head with it." Miles looked mildly ill at the thought. "I don't think it would be an acceptable donation for the silent auction." He added urgently, "And Red said not to tell anyone. So keep it under your hat."

Myrtle said, "You really do need to try and get some sleep. I can't have a sidekick who doesn't feed me information. Didn't you think the murder weapon would be important to divulge?"

Miles said, "We've been with Erma all day. Then you were seeing Sloan. There wasn't really an opportunity to fill you in. Besides, I wasn't supposed to mention it."

Myrtle said impatiently, "Go ahead and fill me in the rest of the way, for heaven's sake. What was the scene like? Did you see any clues?"

Miles wrinkled his forehead in thought and drove a bit slower as he tried to reconstruct what happened this morning. "I knocked on the door and there wasn't any answer."

"Yes, but she'd told you to walk in if she wasn't there. So I'm guessing you didn't spend much time knocking."

Miles said, "No. I tapped on the door another time and then pushed open the door and called out her name, just in case she was there. But there was no answer. I thought she was going to keep the donation near the door, but I didn't see the dog items there, so I started looking for them."

"Did you see anything out of place? Any physical evidence at all?" asked Myrtle.

Miles said, "Well, I wasn't *looking* for physical evidence. I was looking for a dog grooming set and whatnot. Plus, it was kind of dim in there. All the blinds were shut and the curtains were closed. Lillian didn't have any lights turned on. I was mostly just trying not to run into anything in the dark."

Myrtle sighed and Miles continued, "Anyway, I walked into the kitchen and that's when I saw Lillian on the floor. There was blood around her head and on the dog feeding station."

Myrtle said, "When you say *dog feeding station*, I have absolutely no idea what you're talking about. Is this just some sort of a heavy bowl?"

"No, it's a stand that holds a dog bowl and a water bowl. It's pretty big. You wouldn't be able to use it for a short dog—it would be better for a bigger dog. It keeps the dog from having to stoop over the bowl," said Miles.

"So when you found Lillian, did you look around for any clues? Any evidence?" asked Myrtle impatiently.

Miles slowly shook his head. "No. I just made sure there was nothing I could do to help Lillian and then I called for help. And I left the house and tried hard not to be sick. And I wasn't," added Miles with relief.

"I'm glad to hear it," said Myrtle sternly. "But next time when you find a body, try to take better note of your surroundings."

"I'll do my best," said Miles dryly.

Ten minutes later, they were nearing the hubcap-covered shack where Wanda lived with her brother, Crazy Dan off the old highway. The road was now so rarely used that there wasn't much business for the pair's psychic readings, live bait, boiled peanuts, or hubcaps.

Miles said, "And why are we here again? What is it we're trying to find out?"

"I need to ask Wanda if I can mention her in the story I'm writing for Sloan. And I wanted to tell her in person about Lillian's death, since she'd been the one who realized she was in danger," said Myrtle.

"We couldn't have tried to call her on that cell phone Sloan gave her?" asked Miles. He drove onto the red clay of the property and looked around him at the old cars up on cinder blocks and the hubcap-covered shack. His expression was both bemused and dismayed, as it usually was when he encountered Wanda's home.

"She doesn't carry the phone on her. Apparently, she sees it more as a way for her to reach out to the world rather than the other way around," said Myrtle with a shrug as she pushed the car door open.

Myrtle didn't even have the opportunity to knock before Wanda pushed open the dusty screen door and gestured them in.

Myrtle decided it would be nice not to immediately open with the murder. "Hi, Wanda," she said cheerfully. "How are you doing today?"

Wanda gave her a reproachful look. "I done already know."

Miles, never one to accept Wanda's psychic gift outright quickly asked, "Did Sloan call you?"

Wanda gave him a bemused look. "Phone done run out of batteries."

Myrtle frowned at Miles. "You know how she knew. She was the one who said Lillian was in danger to begin with."

Wanda gestured at the meager chairs and waited for them to sit down. Miles, as usual, carefully scoped out all the available options before settling on a seat that might be halfway acceptable. He'd be sure to ask Myrtle for more hand-sanitizer as soon as they left.

When they were seated, Wanda shoved a pile of laundry aside and draped her thin frame over a lumpy loveseat. She shrugged at Myrtle. "Shouldn't have tried to change the future."

Miles said, "What do you mean? That's what you do all the time in your horoscopes. You're always telling people to go to the doctor for their cough or avoid standing on ladders."

Wanda said, "Yeah, but that's small potatoes. With life and death, it's different."

Myrtle said briskly, "Well, it's Lillian's own fault for being so ridiculously foolish. You'd think if someone was trying to tell her something for her own good that she'd listen."

Wanda levelled a look at Myrtle. "Yer in danger."

Myrtle sighed. "I'm well-aware I am. At least I take it seriously."

"But you don't stop nosin' around," said Wanda sadly.

"If you told me I was going to *die*, then I certainly would," said Myrtle. She studied Wanda closely, but the reported danger was apparently not registering on Wanda's psychic radar as fatal because Wanda only shrugged again.

Wanda said, "Got some more horoscopes fer next week."

Myrtle dug around in her purse and produced a notebook and pencil. "All right, shoot." Myrtle much preferred taking down dictation from Wanda instead of trying to decipher the illegible and mostly-illiterate scrawls she'd occasionally hand her.

Miles shifted uncomfortably in his seat and appeared to be on the lookout for any intrepid insects that might be traipsing around Wanda's home.

Wanda drawled, "Frank Wilson needs to change banks. Them fees'll kill him."

Miles raised his eyebrows. "What bank is he with?"

"He'll know," said Wanda.

Myrtle said, "All right. The next one?"

"Let Marian Moore know to jest send her kid to community college. He ain't ready for a big school," she said.

This continued for several more minutes until Wanda finished up. Myrtle carefully put her pencil and notebook back in her purse.

Myrtle said, "There's one other thing I need to ask you, Wanda. Sloan and I thought the article on Lillian might be more interesting for readers if we mentioned the fact you'd made a fateful prediction for her. Would it be all right if I mentioned your name in the story?"

Wanda made a face. "Rather not."

Myrtle said, "Well, I can certainly understand your reluctance. It *is* a crime story, of course." Myrtle preened a little. She enjoyed the prestige of being a crime correspondent. "But remember you're in the paper every week."

"Jest there with the comics," said Wanda dismissively.

"Yes, but with this particular newspaper, everyone turns to the comics first. Nobody can handle the rest of the paper until they've read something funny. And I think a lot of people don't even read the comics first—they go right to your horoscopes. In fact, Sloan has mentioned several times to me that the subscriptions for the paper haven't declined but have actually increased since you've been onboard." Myrtle frowned. "I think he should be giving you some sort of new reader finder's fee. Perhaps he should increase your compensation."

Miles muttered as he glanced nervously around the shack, "For sure."

"Anyway, I completely understand if you *don't* want to be in the story. But I do think it might give your psychic reading business a bit of a boost having your name in a front-page story. Who knows—the article might even be picked up on the wire and other newspapers in other towns might run it," said Myrtle, getting slightly carried away at the thought of her yet-to-be-written piece.

Miles frowned doubtfully at this.

Wanda tilted her head to one side. "Wouldn't mind gettin' more bizness."

"Well, hopefully, and if the people of Bradley have any sense, it will lead to more business. Clearly, I can't make any promises, though. The people of Bradley have proven them-selves foolish on quite a number of occasions," said Myrtle.

Wanda nodded. "Okay. Go ahead and run it."

"Thank you," said Myrtle with a smile. She looked around the shack and said, "Things look great here, by the way." It did. Despite the laundry covering surfaces willy-nilly, there weren't the stacks of clutter on the floor. "Is Crazy Dan not bringing as much stuff inside as he was?"

For a while, Crazy Dan was doing a good imitation of a hoarder. He'd drive by houses on trash day and see what people had left out for the garbage man on the street. Those things would make their way home and end up stacked against the walls, on tables, and in chairs. Myrtle and Miles had helped Wanda make numerous trips to the Goodwill to donate the items and Dan had been bringing things in just as fast as they went out.

"Dan has a new hobby," she drawled.

Miles murmured, "I'm almost afraid to ask what that is."

"Gawfin,'" answered Wanda.

Miles stared at Wanda. "Sorry?"

"Gawfin."

Miles turned to look questioningly at Myrtle.

"For heaven's sake, Miles! Golfing. Pay attention." Myrtle frowned at him.

Miles blinked. "That's rather an expensive hobby, isn't it? Green fees and equipment and all?"

Wanda shook her head. "Naw. He don't play right. Picked up a gawf club off the side of the road and made his own course. Shoots balls into tin cans and scattered them cans all over the yard."

"That's very enterprising of him," said Myrtle. She glanced at her watch. "Well, I suppose we should be heading out. I need to write that article and send it over to Sloan. I'll give him the new horoscopes, too. Thanks for everything, Wanda."

Miles stood up with alacrity. As Myrtle was walking out the door, he pulled his wallet out and surreptitiously gave Wanda some cash. "For a rainy day," he said quickly.

Chapter Five

As Miles drove away, Myrtle said, "Why do I have the feeling that 'golf course' is soon going to be up on their sign along with 'live bait,' 'boiled peanuts,' and 'psychic readings'?"

Miles sighed. "Well, I suppose it's not all that different from miniature golf, if you think about it. At least it was a productive visit, right? You received your permission from Wanda for the news story. And you were warned about imminent danger again."

Myrtle said, "She never said it was *imminent*. I'll simply keep an eye out, as I always do. Now, let's talk about tomorrow morning."

Miles said uncomfortably, "I hope by 'morning' you mean eight o'clock and not four o'clock."

"Technically, four o'clock *is* morning."

"For some people. But not for people who haven't slept for days," said Miles pointedly.

Myrtle said, "I'm not hosting Lieutenant Perkins for breakfast at four o'clock, Miles. But I do think I need to prepare fairly early. For one thing, Puddin hasn't cleaned my house for a ridiculous amount of time."

Puddin was Myrtle's unreliable housekeeper. The only reason Myrtle continued employing her was because her husband, Dusty, was an inexpensive yardman. It was impossible to find inexpensive mowing in Bradley.

Miles said, "What else is new?"

Myrtle frowned. "She's been especially insufferable lately. I'm going to go ahead and call her now, although it will be a pain to have her vacuuming while I'm trying to write my story for Sloan."

She took her phone out of her purse and dialed Puddin's number. Dusty picked up.

"Too dry to mow, Miz Myrtle!" he hollered in the phone. "Not healthy for grass to be cut too short when it's dry."

It was always too wet, too dry, too hot, or too cold for Dusty.

Myrtle said impatiently, "Never mind about that, Dusty. I'm calling for Puddin."

Dusty grunted and called for Puddin. A minute or so went by before Puddin said sullenly, "H'lo?"

"Puddin, it's me. I need you to come by and clean for me."

Puddin growled into the phone, "My back is thrown, Miz Myrtle."

Myrtle said, "Absolutely not. That was your excuse for the last two weeks. And the last time I went to my internist, he told me in no uncertain terms that a back can be *helped* by moderate activity."

Puddin paused and then said, "Speak English, Miz Myrtle."

"He said you should clean for me. Now come on over. I have guests tomorrow morning for breakfast and no time for your foolishness."

Puddin drawled, "Have to see if the car will start."

"Well, if it doesn't, then take Dusty's truck. It sure doesn't sound as if he'll be using it since he says it's too dry to mow anyone's grass," said Myrtle with a sniff. "I'll see you at the house in thirty minutes." She hung up the phone.

Miles said, "About this breakfast tomorrow. You're just planning on eggs and bacon and grits, right? Maybe some cereal?" His voice sounded hopeful.

"Absolutely not! That would be pedestrian and predictable. Perkins is a hard-working police detective and he deserves something special. I was thinking about making quiches. Or eggs benedict. Or maybe even a soufflé."

Miles gave her an anxious sidelong look and Myrtle snapped, "Eyes on the road, Miles! We don't need to have an accident just a few blocks from home."

Miles stared back at the road in front of him. "I think that's taking on a lot, Myrtle. You have a front-page story to write for Sloan. You have to keep Puddin on track with her cleaning and make sure she's not watching TV instead of working. Besides, you probably don't even have all the ingredients you need for these fancy breakfast recipes."

Myrtle waved a hand in the air. "Sure, I do. It's just eggs and stuff. Those are staples at my house and Red just drove me to the store a few days ago. Besides, if there's an ingredient I'm short on, I can just substitute something else. That's what cooking is all about—creativity. And I'm a creative person."

Miles sighed. Then he said quickly, "What can I bring over? Guests are supposed to bring over contributions, after all."

Myrtle said doubtfully, "Do they do that for a breakfast? I'm not really sure about that. That's more of a dinner thing where maybe they bring over a bottle of wine."

"Perhaps it would be good to serve alcohol tomorrow," muttered Miles.

"No, no, it's way too early. Besides, Perkins has to go off to work immediately afterwards. It's far too early even for mimosas or bloody Marys. I suppose, if you must bring something, perhaps a bread of some kind. That might work well. But I don't want Perkins to feel uncomfortable if *he* doesn't bring anything, so be sure to be unobtrusive when you bring it in."

"I'll try," said Miles.

Myrtle was furiously writing her story for Sloan when she heard a loud vehicle rattling up in front of her house. She peeked out the window to see Dusty's truck with Puddin's pale, pasty, unhappy face behind the wheel. She opened the door and waited as Puddin slouched unhappily up the front walk.

Myrtle glared at her. "Where are your cleaning supplies, Puddin?"

Puddin glared back. "Don't got 'em, do I? I'm in Dusty's truck. He don't got no cleaners."

"I don't have time today for this nonsense. You should have grabbed your supplies from your car before you got into Dusty's truck."

Puddin raised her eyebrows. "You tole me to come right away."

Myrtle gestured Puddin inside. "For heaven's sake. You'd try the patience of a saint. Just come on in and use my cleaning supplies, like you usually do anyway."

"Them supplies is expensive," muttered Puddin sullenly.

"Yes, I *know*," said Myrtle. "That's my point. Never mind. You get started with the cleaning. I've got to finish this article and send it over to Sloan . . . I have a deadline."

Puddin, naturally, picked the loudest activity to start with so she could be at the maximum level of being annoying. The vacuum cleaner roared back and forth beside Myrtle, being shoved around by a resentful Puddin. Myrtle put headphones on and gritted her teeth as she continued to write the story.

At some point, the roaring stopped and Myrtle continued to write, headphones on and soft music playing. But when she finally noticed it was far too quiet in her house, she took the headphones off and looked around the room. She saw Puddin sitting on her sofa, talking on the phone.

"Puddin!" hissed Myrtle.

Puddin said in annoyance, "One minute, Miz Myrtle."

"I think you've already had that," muttered Myrtle.

Puddin ignored her. "All right. All right, Bitsy. I'll be right over there. Yep, got the truck."

Puddin hung up and Myrtle stared coldly at her. "I hope by 'be right over,' you meant in two hours. You haven't even finished vacuuming the house, Puddin!"

Puddin shrugged. "Can't do it, Miz Myrtle. That was my cousin Bitsy."

"Yes, I gathered it was one of your various and sundry cousins. What did she want?"

Puddin said, "She threw her back and needs a ride to the doctor."

Myrtle closed her eyes and then slowly opened them. "Surely, thrown backs aren't contagious."

Puddin shrugged. "Maybe it's one of them genetic things."

"Maybe you could simply advise her on it, since you experience them so frequently yourself," said Myrtle smoothly.

Puddin screwed up her face. "Don't like it when you don't speak English, Miz Myrtle. Anyway, gotta go. See you later."

"Later *when*?" demanded Myrtle.

But Puddin had already gone, leaving the vacuum in the middle of the floor.

Myrtle muttered dire imprecations about the complete unreliability of Puddins in general and glanced around the small living room. She supposed it would appear clean enough if she kept the lighting fairly low. Would it be odd to dine by candlelight at seven-thirty in the morning? Regardless, she didn't have any time to worry with it all. She needed to finish her story for Sloan and then get things ready for Perkins to come over tomorrow. She wanted to put out a fresh tablecloth in the kitchen and use her better china. She just needed to make sure her better china wasn't dusty from disuse.

It took her quite a bit longer to do these things than she'd thought. But that was because Tippy called once again to speak to her and fret about the silent auction and the suitability of having it go on as planned or politely shelving it for another date. Myrtle had been tapping her foot through the entire phone conversation until she was finally able to get Tippy off the phone. She was worried Sloan had either forgotten about her story or had given up on it for the day, so gave him a follow-up call to let him know she had just emailed it to him ten minutes after she'd gotten off the phone with Tippy.

"By the way, you need to give Wanda a raise," said Myrtle.

There was a pause on the other end of the line. "Why do you say that?" Sloan's voice was cautious.

"Think of all the attention she brings for the paper. You'd told me yourself subscriptions were up and that simply doesn't happen for newspapers these days. Since Wanda is such a draw, she should have a cut of the profits."

Sloan said, "Miss Myrtle, we're not really drowning in profits here. We're barely keeping our heads above water."

"So is Wanda," said Myrtle sharply.

Sloan sounded miserable as he always did when he had to contradict Myrtle. "Miss Myrtle, I'm just not really sure that's feasible."

"I see." Myrtle pursed her lips. "I didn't want to do this, Sloan, but I happen to have a transcribed horoscope column from Wanda in my possession right this very minute. It has gobs of information your subscribers are going to want to see. But I don't feel right hitting 'send' on the email until I have your word you're going to increase Wanda's compensation."

There was a groan on the other end.

Myrtle snapped, "I don't have time to play games. It's time for me to turn in since I have a busy day tomorrow. But I'm sure there'll be a lot of disappointed people when there's no horoscope in the paper."

A moment later Sloan quickly offered to increase Wanda's salary by five percent. Myrtle smiled and sent the email.

Finally, she dropped into bed and, surprisingly, slept very soundly.

Chapter Six

The next morning, Myrtle rose rather late—past four o'clock. She hurried to the window to see if the newspaper was there. Spotting it, she rushed outside to make sure her story was on the front page. It was. Sloan had even found a photo in his archives of Lillian's flower shop to accompany it. And Wanda's horoscopes made it in too, of course. In Sloan's eyes, that was possibly the more important piece to include.

Myrtle carefully set the paper on the kitchen table, where her story could be easily seen. Then she pulled out one of her old cookbooks and searched for soufflés in the index.

"Miles was wrong," she muttered to herself. "Just basic stuff in these things. Butter, eggs, flour, milk, salt, nutmeg." She paused. There were quite a lot of eggs in this particular recipe. She checked her fridge. She'd simply have to be a couple of eggs short.

Myrtle glanced at the recipe again. What on earth was comtè cheese? "This recipe is no good," she murmured. She walked into the living room to pull up another recipe off the internet. But she found the internet was surprisingly unobliging. It prompted her to use gruyère cheese or grated parmesan. She

49

was pretty sure she had emptied the can of parmesan the last time she'd had spaghetti. Myrtle strode back into the kitchen and looked in the fridge. It appeared she only had a loaf of processed cheese. Velveeta would have to do.

Fifteen minutes later, Myrtle remembered that not only was she to prepare breakfast for Lt. Perkins, she was also supposed to concoct a casserole for Lillian's son. And perhaps her daughter. The nice thing about casseroles was that you could sort of make them up as you went along.

"Let's see. A protein, a vegetable, and a carb. And cream of something soup," muttered Myrtle. The only problem was the only protein she had was solid as a rock in her freezer. Red and she had just gone to the store, but apparently they'd picked up all the wrong things. She snapped her fingers. She had all those cans of tuna in the pantry. She pulled out a few of them and then considered the vegetable. The frozen chopped spinach packets in the freezer would be messy and maybe watery once they defrosted. But if she put extra carbs in the casserole, it should absorb the excess liquid.

Her mind made up, Myrtle pulled the spinach out of the freezer. There was really nothing to cooking. She didn't understand why people struggled so much with it. When it came to the carb for the casserole, however, she discovered she had only a few uncooked spaghetti noodles and about a quarter cup of rice. The store wasn't close to being open yet, and Miles would likely fuss if she called him this early to borrow something. Myrtle frowned and then opened her freezer. There she found a bag of French fries, the really skinny kind. Figuring a carb was a carb, she heated up the oven to cook them. They could line the bottom of the dish.

The only problem, Myrtle decided later, was that she had too many things cooking at once. The milk for the soufflé, which was supposed to be steaming, was boiling instead. The French fries had gotten quite crisp while Myrtle had been attending to whisking flour into the over-hot milk. She realized in the middle of the whisking process that she'd been intended to whisk the flour into some melted *butter* and the milk was supposed to stay separate until later. The frozen spinach appeared to want to stay frozen at all costs and was not cooperating whatsoever in the melting process in the microwave.

She must have lost track of time because she was surprised when there was a knock at the door. She hurried over and let Miles in.

"You're a little early, aren't you?" she asked as she hurried back to the kitchen.

"Only by twenty minutes. You wanted me to be unobtrusive with my donation for the breakfast, remember?" He lay a bag down on the kitchen table that appeared to be overflowing with bread.

"That's quite a lot of bread," said Myrtle. "There are only three of us, remember?"

Miles said, "I figured too much was better than not having enough." He took a seat at the kitchen table and then looked over at the stove with trepidation. "What's going on over there?"

Myrtle peered into the saucepan. "For some reason, the mixture turned brown." She shrugged. "It's all chemistry, you know, Miles. Some sort of chemical reaction happened."

"With our breakfast," said Miles slowly. He shifted uncomfortably in his seat.

"Miles, I really don't have time to talk about this right now. I have a casserole being constructed alongside the soufflé. And now I'm supposed to use the electric mixer on the eggs."

Miles glanced at the counter. "Where is the recipe you're following?"

"It's in my head," said Myrtle, tapping her forehead before pulling out her mixer from a cabinet.

Miles frowned. "For the soufflé? It's not as if you cook those all the time."

Myrtle sighed. "I looked up the recipe on the internet and paid very careful attention to it."

Miles shifted again in his seat. "Is the recipe still up on the screen? I might print it out."

"Why on earth would you want to do that? I've got this all under control."

Miles considered his answer to this carefully. "I might like a copy of it to take home. Maybe I'll cook a soufflé myself sometime."

Myrtle looked doubtful at this, but shrugged. "Suit yourself. The recipe is still up on the computer."

Miles quickly returned with the printed recipe in under a minute. Myrtle was busily mixing the eggs as Miles peered over her shoulder.

"It says here," he said loudly over the roar of the mixer, "that you're only supposed to beat the egg *whites*."

Myrtle looked into the bowl at the eggs. "Well, that's just for people who are trying to lose weight," she hollered over the mixer. "Lt. Perkins is always very trim."

Miles studied the printed recipe. "I don't think that's why you're supposed to use the egg whites. It says here that the egg whites are supposed to get stiff. I don't think that will happen with the whole eggs."

Myrtle said, "Don't be a worrywart, Miles. It will be fine. And the soufflé will have extra protein."

She stopped the mixer and said, "Now I should add the cheese."

Miles glanced at the recipe again. "Gruyère."

Myrtle gave him an impatient look. "Or not."

He looked back at the recipe. "It doesn't say 'or not.'"

Myrtle said, "Yes, but everyone knows the point is to be creative."

"I thought the point was to eat something tasty," said Miles slowly.

"Which we will be. Look, the reason the recipe says gruyere is because that's one of those cheeses that melts well," said Myrtle.

"I'm rather impressed you knew that," said Miles thoughtfully.

"Sure. It's in all those croque madams or croque monsieurs or whatever it is the French eat that's like a grilled cheese. Anyway, the idea is simply to put a cheese in that melts really well."

Miles now glanced at the fridge with concern. "I'm a little afraid to ask what cheese you decided was up to this challenge."

She shrugged. "It's obvious, isn't it? Velveeta. Processed cheese melts much better than any kind of French cheese. And it's made in the USA."

Miles walked to the fridge and removed the Velveeta. He carefully read the box the cheese was in. "Technically, Velveeta isn't cheese at all."

"Of course it is, Miles! Don't be difficult. Everyone uses it for cheese dips, for heaven's sake."

"But not, perhaps, for soufflés," said Miles stiffly. He turned and looked longingly at Myrtle's front door. He turned back and said, "It says here on the box that it's 'Pasteurized Prepared Food Product.'"

"You're being such a stickler. The fact of the matter is that it's cheesy. It will lend the taste of cheese to the soufflé. That's all I'm looking for."

Miles rubbed his eyes.

Myrtle said crossly, "And please fix yourself some coffee. It looks like you didn't sleep last night again and I can't have you dropping off to sleep in front of Perkins as if my breakfast was boring or something. I'm putting too much time into this meal." She frowned and looked at the casserole for Lillian's son and daughter. "Let's see. The casserole should go in at 350 degrees and the soufflé was something like 400 degrees."

Miles gazed hopelessly at the oven.

"It's best to compromise in situations like these and set it for 375 degrees," said Myrtle decisively as she set the temperature.

Twenty minutes later, there was a light tap at the front door. Miles leapt up. "I'll get it," he said, rushing for the door as Myrtle opened the oven door and frowned at the soufflé.

There were words exchanged between Miles and Perkins in a low voice and then Perkins walked into the kitchen with a bright smile. Myrtle gave him a hug, which always knocked Perkins somewhat off-balance.

"Good morning!" she said, beaming at him. "I'm so glad you've made it for breakfast. Can I get you a cup of coffee? We actually have a few minutes to talk because this soufflé hasn't risen yet." She glared at the oven as if the soufflé was being intentionally difficult.

"A cup of coffee would be wonderful," said Perkins, folding himself into one of Myrtle's kitchen chairs. "I just take it black. This is so nice of you, Mrs. Clover. And the table looks beautiful."

Myrtle smiled at him again. "I can tell your mama raised you well. I thought this was definitely an occasion for my nice china. I've wanted to have you over for a meal for so long."

She brought over the coffee and sat next to him. "I'm just glad you were able to find the time to come over with everything going on. Tell me all about how things are going with the case."

Perkins said mildly, "Now, Mrs. Clover, you know I can't really discuss police business with you."

"Oh, pooh. You can make an exception in my case, surely! You know how many cases I've helped you and Red solve. I'm practically indispensable."

Miles cocked an eyebrow at her.

Perkins said, "You have definitely been helpful in the past, but I'm still somewhat constricted in terms of what I'm allowed to say. Tell you what—ask me a question and I'll see if I'm able to answer it."

"Do you know who did it?" asked Myrtle with an innocent smile.

Perkins gave a slight smile. "Not yet."

"Was there any physical evidence left behind?"

Perkins said, "Unfortunately, there have been plenty of people in the victim's house. It does make the physical evidence a challenge. But to answer your question, there was no smoking gun, so to speak, in terms of forensic evidence or other evidence."

Myrtle frowned. "These criminals certainly are getting sneaky."

Miles said anxiously, "Should you check the soufflé again?"

"I swear, you've been quite fretful over this breakfast. It looked as if it had a few more minutes . . . it hadn't risen." Myrtle turned back to Perkins with a sweet smile. "Besides the family, who might be the most-likely suspects?"

His lips quirked and then he said, "Unfortunately, that's information I can't reveal."

"Was it only one attacker or were there more than one?"

Perkins said, "That's confidential information, I'm afraid."

"What were the terms of Lillian's will?"

Perkins gave her an admiring look. "That would be something else I can't answer."

Myrtle paused. "Would you like another cup of coffee?"

"That would be marvelous, thank you, Mrs. Clover."

Myrtle walked back to the coffeemaker and vigorously made him a coffee, this time with lots of cream and sugar. He took it without complaint, drinking an experimental sip.

Miles pushed his chair back. "I'll volunteer to check on the soufflé."

Myrtle rolled her eyes as Miles opened the oven door and peered solicitously inside. He grimaced. "I don't think the soufflé will be rising anytime soon. But it needs to come out."

"If it hasn't risen, it shouldn't come out," said Myrtle crossly.

"It's starting to burn. And there's no sign of it rising."

Pasha looked in through the kitchen window and Myrtle absently shoved it open and fixed Pasha's breakfast. "Well, that's very odd. Let's go ahead and eat it, then, if it's trying to burn. It'll *taste* the same, after all, even if it doesn't look like it's supposed to."

Miles appeared doubtful on this point. He and Perkins exchanged glances.

Pasha stared unblinkingly at the oven.

Myrtle got out her rooster-themed oven mitts and carefully took out the soufflé. She studied it through the glass dish. "That's very odd. It's done on the top and liquidy on the bottom."

Miles closed his eyes briefly.

Perkins said smoothly, "Isn't there a French breakfast dish like that? Sort of a custard?"

Myrtle said in a thoughtful voice, "I believe you might be right. Well, we're going to have an international-themed breakfast."

Miles looked suspiciously at the quasi-soufflé. "Is it safe to eat uncooked eggs?"

"People eat custards all the time," said Myrtle with a shrug.

"Aren't the custards *set*, though? Aren't they more of a solid?" Miles watched with horror as the custard sloshed around the bottom of the glass bowl as Myrtle placed it on the kitchen table with a flourish.

"Ta-da!" she said, ignoring Miles's questions.

Perkins said, "May I slice the soufflé?"

Myrtle beamed at him. "You may have the honor!"

The top of the soufflé/custard was quite firm indeed. Myrtle had to fish a steak knife out of a drawer and Perkins sawed vigorously at the breakfast dish for several minutes before serving the three of them a slice each. He looked at the bottom of the bowl at the nebulous liquid. "It's very cheesy," he said politely.

"Maybe we should pour the custard part on the top of our soufflé slices," said Myrtle, feeling very innovative. "I should really post this recipe online with all of my substitutions."

Miles muttered something unintelligible under his breath while Perkins carefully drizzled the cheesy custard on the top of the crunchy soufflé slices.

Pasha took this opportunity to leap onto the counter and back out the kitchen window as if concerned some of the soufflé might end up in her own bowl.

"Bon Appetit!" said Myrtle cheerily as she sawed off a mouthful of the soufflé.

Miles cut off the smallest possible taste of the breakfast dish and gazed at his fork with immense distrust before delicately putting a bite in his mouth. He quickly brought his napkin to his mouth and unobtrusively deposited the mouthful into its welcoming depths.

Perkins was apparently made of sterner stuff. He swallowed his bite of food, praised Myrtle's cooking and effort, and then continued eating with discipline and determination.

Myrtle took a thoughtful bite. "It's rather rich, isn't it?"

"Very filling," agreed Perkins. "It's good we had small slices."

Miles looked miserably at his slice, which wasn't going to become any smaller than it already was, and willed it to disappear.

Myrtle said, "And perhaps it needs something. Do you think it needs something, Perkins?"

Perkins smiled tightly at her. "I think it's quite perfect the way it is right now."

Myrtle gave a contented sigh. Then she glanced over at Miles. "What's going on, Miles? Are you unwell?"

Miles pressed his lips together and then said, "It might be that the lack of sleep is catching up with me."

"And affecting your appetite?" asked Myrtle with a frown.

Miles shrugged. "I'm not a medical person."

"I thought you'd have picked up some medical information after all your years in hospital administration," said Myrtle.

Miles gave her a cold look. "I was an engineer."

Perkins's lips twitched. Then he quickly said, "Mrs. Clover, I'm interested in the work you've done for the newspaper. It looks like you have a front-page story today. Could you tell me all about it?"

Myrtle preened, launching into a narrative about her role at the newspaper while Miles continued pushing his soufflé incrementally farther away from him. Perkins cleaned his plate.

As Myrtle started wrapping up her story, Miles broke in. "Myrtle, is something burning?"

"The soufflé is here on the table," said Myrtle crossly.

"Is there anything *else* in the oven?" asked Miles.

Myrtle snapped her fingers. "The casserole!"

She put on her rooster oven mitts again and reached into the oven, pulling out the casserole. Myrtle studied it carefully and then said, "Oh, it's just fine. It's simply nice and firm."

Pasha stared at the oven distastefully from outside the window as thin black smoke wafted toward her.

Myrtle frowned. "But I think I forgot an ingredient."

"Which one?" asked Miles.

Perkins's shoulders appeared to shake for a moment before he quickly got himself under control again.

"The cream-of-something," she muttered, still evaluating the casserole.

"Cream?" asked Miles. "In a casserole?"

"No, cream-of-something *soup*. You can choose mushroom, chicken, cheese, or broccoli. It never really matters which one. But I didn't mix it in," said Myrtle.

Perkins stood up and walked over to gaze at the casserole in question. "I think you could smooth it on top, couldn't you? It would almost be like cake icing since the casserole itself is so firm."

Myrtle gave him an approving look. "Excellent point, Lt. Perkins!"

Perkins glanced down as his cell phone rang. "Excuse me."

He picked up and said, "Perkins. Oh, hi, Red." He listened for a moment. "No, everything is fine." He gave Myrtle a reassuring smile since Myrtle had immediately become grouchy at the mention of Red. "All right. Yes, I'll be right over."

He put his phone back in his pocket and gave Myrtle and Miles an apologetic smile. "I'm afraid I have to get going. Thanks so much for the lovely breakfast, Mrs. Clover. It was good to see both of you."

He picked up his plate, rinsed it, and put it carefully into the dishwasher.

"Bread for the road?" asked Miles with alacrity, shoving a plate of croissants at him.

"Thanks," said Perkins quickly, grabbing a couple before giving Myrtle another smile and heading swiftly out the door.

Chapter Seven

"Well, that was very nice," said Myrtle.

Miles merely gave a relieved sigh.

"He really is such a nice young man. I'm glad I finally had the chance to have him over for a meal. I should do this every time."

Miles closed his eyes briefly. "Can I help you clean up?" he asked.

Myrtle looked around the kitchen and made a face. "I've half a mind to drag Puddin back over here and have her do it. It's amazing how a couple of simple recipes can make for so much mess. Puddin definitely owes me one. That silly Bitsy called and Puddin didn't even have the chance to do any cleaning at all."

Miles looked at the clock. "I'd say your chances of getting Puddin over here at this time of the morning are slim to none."

"It's not even that early anymore! But I know what you mean. Puddin is so slovenly, she probably is still buried under the covers." Myrtle looked at the clock, herself. "I think we should head over to Martin's house with the casserole. I'll just have the dishes sit in some dish soap for a while. That should make clean-up easier for either me or Puddin."

Miles said, "Are you sure Martin wants to be faced with a casserole at this point of the morning?"

"*Faced* with it? What a peculiar turn of phrase, Miles. And, yes, I think he would want it early so he could even have it for lunch if he wanted. Or he could have it for lunch *and* supper."

"Weren't you going to divide it up so we could give some to Lillian's daughter, as well? It made an awful lot?"

Indeed, the casserole completely filled a large dish. It was also quite dense, somehow, and heavy.

"Yes, I think it should be divided up. I think we'd have a hard time even trying to hold the thing in one container. That way, we can see Annie right after we see Martin." Myrtle studied the casserole. "I'm going to need you to help me transfer the thing over. It looks like it might be unmanageable." She glared at the casserole as if it were being purposefully obstructive.

"Do you have a couple of containers that will work?" asked Miles. "It's kind of a rectangular shape."

Myrtle pulled open a cabinet and frowned as she surveyed the different plastic options. "This one is sort of a rectangle."

"It's a square," said Miles.

"It couldn't be. It's shorter on these sides."

Miles said, "It's exactly the same on all sides."

Myrtle sniffed. "If you really *were* an engineer, it seems as if you should know your shapes a bit better."

Miles said tightly, "May I have a look in your cabinet?"

The cabinet was a riot of orphaned lids and containers. Some of them appeared to be from old butter containers, others from hummus. Most of them didn't seem to be appropriate for transporting casseroles to the bereaved.

"I have some containers at home," said Miles. "I'll be right back."

He returned a few minutes later with a couple of rectangular plastic containers. "These should do the job," he said.

They struggled a bit with the transferal process. The casserole was decidedly uncooperative. Both of them wielded spatulas and finally just wrestled the mixture into place.

Miles stared down glumly at the two containers when they'd finished. "It doesn't look very good."

"But I'm about to cover them with the cream-of-something soup," said Myrtle. "You won't be able to tell how broken up the casserole is once I smooth the soup over it."

Miles looked less-certain. "Is this chicken in the casserole?" he asked suspiciously.

"Tuna. Lots of protein," said Myrtle.

Miles didn't look any happier.

Myrtle said thoughtfully, "Come to think of it, perhaps that's why Pasha happened by. She could smell the tuna cooking. Darling Pasha. She's so very bright!"

Myrtle opened a can of cream of broccoli soup and carefully spread it over the various pieces of casserole in the containers while Miles looked on. Then she lay them in the bottom of plastic bags and said, "That's it, then. Let's head out."

"Where are we going first?" asked Miles a minute later as he backed his car out of Myrtle's driveway.

"Let's talk to Lillian's son. Martin will hopefully be able to give us some sort of information."

"What's he like?" asked Miles a bit nervously. "Is he the sort of man who will be upset at having his doorbell rung very early? Or at receiving a container of tuna casserole before breakfast?"

Myrtle gave him a sharp look. "Certainly not! He's very gregarious. He's in sales of some sort, I think. From what Lillian has said, anyway. I haven't seen the man in years."

"Pharmaceuticals? Real estate?"

"Insurance, I believe," said Myrtle.

Miles looked even gloomier. "I'm frequently a target of insurance salesmen. They always seem to think I don't have proper coverage."

A few minutes later, they arrived at Martin's house.

Miles raised his eyebrows as he drove down the driveway. "This place is tremendous. Martin lives alone here?"

"That's what I understand," said Myrtle with a shrug.

"And he has this huge property . . . on the lake . . . from selling insurance?"

Myrtle said, "Unless he has family money of some sort."

"His mother owned a flower shop!"

Myrtle said, "Maybe he won the lottery or something. Who knows?"

"Or maybe he's been living beyond his means," said Miles.

They rang the doorbell and waited. There was no answer.

Myrtle frowned. "Maybe the doorbell isn't working."

"Or maybe he's asleep," said Miles dryly.

Myrtle rang the bell again and then rapped briskly at the front door. Finally, the door opened and a bleary-eyed man in his thirties gazed sleepily at them. He looked at the bag Myrtle carried with confusion. "Can I help you?" he asked.

Myrtle gave him a sad smile. "Martin, you may not remember me because it's been many years since I've seen you. I'm Myrtle Clover and this is my friend Miles Bradford. We were friends of your mother's."

Martin didn't immediately seem to remember Myrtle, but his natural affable manner started coming through as he woke up. "Of course," he said, beaming at them both. "Please come inside. I hope you'll forgive my appearance—I had a rather long day yesterday and I'm afraid I'm getting something of a later start."

Myrtle and Miles followed him in. They stood in a massive stone atrium that made their voices echo. Martin clearly ascribed to a minimalist style of decorating because there wasn't much in the way of furniture, art, or even photographs in the rooms nearby.

Myrtle said, "We were so sorry to hear about your poor mother. Miles and I have brought you a casserole for later."

Miles said emphatically, "Actually, it's Myrtle's casserole. I just wanted to express my condolences in person."

Martin said, "Thank you both so much. You're very thoughtful. Please have a seat for a few minutes." He gestured into the living room and they perched on a silk sofa as Martin sat down in a very modern looking Swedish-influenced armchair that didn't seem to go with the antique sofa at all.

Martin said, "How did you know Mama?"

Myrtle said, "Oh, Miles and I are in garden club with Lillian. Lillian, of course, is such a plant expert with her florist business. We loved hearing her talk about different types of native plants and flower arranging. Didn't we, Miles?"

Miles shifted uncomfortably on the sofa. He hadn't really known Lillian well at all and had just joined garden club. He nodded, giving Martin a tight smile.

Martin looked thoughtful for a moment. "Wait a minute. Miles. I want to say the police chief said a gentleman named Miles had found Mama yesterday morning. Was that you?" he asked of Miles.

Miles now looked even more uncomfortable. "I'm afraid so. I'm very sorry," he said miserably as if the entire problem would have been avoided if he simply hadn't been at Lillian's house the previous morning.

"I'm sorry for you," said Martin. "That must have been pretty awful." He paused. "The police chief didn't mention why you were there." His voice was curious.

Miles flushed and spluttered a bit until Myrtle cut in smoothly, "The police chief is my son, Red, as a matter of fact. He can be rather absentminded sometimes. Miles was there to collect your mother's donation for the silent auction the club is having."

A spark of remembrance crossed Martin's features. "Ah. Now that you mention it, I do remember Mama talking about the silent auction. Her donation had something to do with dogs, didn't it?"

Myrtle nodded. "That's right. Actually, one of the reasons I'm here is to ask you about the auction. Our garden club president, Tippy, was most concerned about Lillian's death. She didn't want to proceed with the auction if it might bring any discomfort or sadness at all to you or your sister."

Martin raised an eyebrow and then lowered it again. He gave them a big smile. "I appreciate Tippy's concern. But then, she's always seemed like a really thoughtful person. Mama thought she was, at least. But I don't think there's anything in the slightest that would upset either Annie or myself about the garden club silent auction."

Miles's eyes were amused as if he'd half-expected as much.

Myrtle said, "I'm sure Tippy is going to give some sort of tribute to your Mama at the event, too. We're all sorry Lillian will no longer be part of our group. And I'm sure Tippy would want me to extend an invitation to both of you to the auction."

Martin said, "That's very kind of you. I'll be sure to check in with Annie and see if that's something we're able to do." He shook his head. "The whole thing still seems totally unbelievable to me. Who on earth would kill Mama? And your son doesn't appear to believe it's a break-in. Why would someone want to kill a florist?"

"Why indeed?" said Myrtle, tilting her head to one side and looking at Martin.

He paused for a moment and then said, "Although Mama could be strong-willed. She was also very particular about things and could be hard on a person if she perceived they had faults. Do people really commit murder over a perceived wrong?"

Miles cleared his throat. "Maybe. Maybe it depends on the wrong."

"Even something very silly? Because small-town grievances can be really petty. Take, for instance, Mama's neighbor. Have you met her?" Martin asked them.

They shook their heads.

Martin said, "Mama and she have been in something of a spat. I have absolutely no idea what it's over, but it's guaranteed to be something ridiculous. Mama told me about it, but I can't for the life of me remember what it was all about." He absently reached out to the coffee table in front of his chair and picked up a sterling silver business card holder and started fidgeting with it.

Myrtle, having been a schoolteacher for many years, was never fond of fidgeting. She stifled a sigh and said, "Did you mention the neighbor to Red?"

Martin flipped the card holder into the air and caught it. "No. It just seemed like something so innocuous. I didn't want to tie up police time by having them chase a false lead."

Myrtle said, "I'd think it's one of those things that wouldn't immediately come to mind anyway, would it? After the shock of the bad news."

"That's true. I just started thinking about the neighbor when I finally turned in last night. I can't even remember the woman's name. Medea or Valentina or something. Sort of exotic."

Miles looked surprised, remembering the rather pedestrian appearance of the neighbor chatting with Erma. "The neighbor is exotic?"

"No, her name is," said Martin.

"Oh, I think I remember Erma telling me the neighbor's name. Tallulah, wasn't it?" asked Myrtle.

Martin nodded. "That's it. Anyway, you're right about the shock. I don't know if I've quite shaken it. I'd been sleeping in yesterday morning after fishing all day the day before."

Myrtle frowned. "Are the fish biting when it's this hot? I thought they'd be at the bottom of the lake trying to stay cool."

Martin looked surprised and then gave her an admiring look. "I can tell you've lived on a lake for a while."

"Eighty or more years," said Myrtle casually.

Martin said, "Well, I could have used your advice day-before-yesterday because the fish were *not* biting. They weren't even considering it. I was out there early in the morning and then went in around lunchtime and came back out again by mid-afternoon. I was out there until right before sunset. Didn't catch a single fish. Although I did relax, and that was something I really needed. Had a few drinks, chilled out with the fishing pole."

Myrtle said, "I'd imagine that being in the sun all day would be very exhausting."

Martin pointed the silver business card holder and said, "Bingo! Yes, it was. I came home, fishless, and had a microwave meal for supper. Pretty pathetic, since I'd thought I'd be cleaning fish and having a wonderful fish dinner. Then I could barely keep my eyes open when I was watching TV, so turned in early. I slept until the police knocked on my door yesterday morning." He shook his head. "I'm going to miss Mama. She and I were very close. There's something special about a mother and son relationship, isn't there?"

"Is there?" asked Myrtle archly, thinking darkly about Red.

Martin chuckled, "Well, in my case there was, anyway. I just can't believe she's gone. She was so health-conscious that I'd always thought she'd outlive me."

Miles asked, "What will become of the shop?"

Martin sighed. "I suppose I'll be the owner of a flower shop. I'm running by there later today to check in. This whole thing is going to be a mess." Despite whatever mess Martin thought might be involved in only a flower shop, Myrtle noted his eyes lit up with greed for a moment.

Miles asked, "You mean, you and your sister will own it?"

Martin fumbled the silver card holder, nearly dropping it. "Of course. Annie and me."

"How is your sister handling everything?" asked Myrtle. "You're both awfully young to be losing your mother. We have some food for her, too. Is there anything else we can do for her?"

Martin's eyes narrowed for a moment. "She's taking it all pretty hard, actually. She and Mama would scrap all the time over silly stuff, but that's pretty natural with mothers and daughters, isn't it? The problem is that she and Mama had words, as usual, and Mama died before Annie had the chance to make up with her. I think she's sick over it. I know she'll appreciate the food."

"Is she in town?" asked Myrtle. "I'd heard she might be moving? Something like that?"

"Annie *wanted* to move, yes. But she's still in an apartment here in Bradley. Mama was trying to make her work in the flower shop, but Annie had bigger ideas." Martin shrugged. "Actually, I *might* be the sole owner of the shop."

"Do you know much about arranging flowers?" asked Myrtle, quirking an eyebrow.

"Ah. No, I don't. I'll have to hire a florist." This detail had apparently not occurred to Martin before now. "Perhaps it would be best to just sell the shop's real estate. Plenty of time to figure that out, though." He paused and then said, "You know, all of this business with poor Mama had gotten me to thinking about the shortness and fragility of life."

Miles looked alarmed and shifted in his chair.

"That's one reason why I have such good life insurance—to ensure my family won't have to go into debt for my funeral and other expenses," added Martin smoothly. "You may not know this, but I'm in the insurance business. This tragedy might provide a very natural time to evaluate the coverage you have."

Miles spluttered that he had *lots* of insurance. Martin looked doubtfully at him. Myrtle said offhandedly that she was set for insurance.

"But are you sure you are?" pressed Martin. "There's nothing like peace of mind when it comes to insurance. You don't have to worry about your loved ones struggling after you're gone."

Myrtle's voice was complacent, "I don't worry. They'll be just fine."

Martin started wheedling. "Maybe you're set with life insurance, but you might be surprised to find how inexpensive some vital insurance can be. Take roofing insurance, for example. You know how expensive it can be to replace an entire roof. It's outrageous! And we do get some really extreme weather in this section of the country. All we need is another hailstorm and you'll need to spend a lot of money to put a roof over your head."

"That's what homeowner's insurance is for," said Myrtle placidly. "Which I have."

"Yes, but homeowner's insurance might not always come through. There are certain conditions that have to be met. You'd be amazed to hear there is roofing insurance available for only seventeen dollars a month."

Myrtle shook her head, a slight smile around her lips. Miles looked longingly at the front door.

Martin continued, "Hail can also do a lot of damage to windows. The cost of window replacement is steadily climbing, but you can get a special rider with my company for only four dollars a month." He looked archly at Myrtle.

Myrtle said with a laugh, "Martin, you are quite the salesman. But what you don't know is that I'm on a fixed income. There is absolutely no way on this green earth you'll be able to convince me to add a recurring charge to my regular expenses."

Martin looked flummoxed for a moment and then gave a hearty laugh. "A lady who likes to take her chances! Well, that's just fine. You know who to see if you ever change your mind." He reached into the silver business card holder and handed Myrtle his card.

Myrtle took it with a sweet smile and stuck it into the depths of her cavernous purse.

Miles said to Myrtle, "Perhaps we should leave, Myrtle. I'm sure Martin has a busy day ahead of him."

Martin stood and said, "Yes, planning a service for poor Mama. At least there will be beautiful flowers there—when I run by the shop, I'll have Bianca make some really special arrangements."

"Do you know when the service will be held?" asked Myrtle. She knew from past experiences that she needed to make sure her funeral outfit was in good condition.

"Not yet, but the police didn't think they'd need Mama for very long. I'm hoping in a couple of days," said Martin.

They walked to the front door and Martin said, "Thanks again for the casserole. That's very thoughtful of you both."

Miles said in a somewhat strangled voice, "It's Myrtle's casserole, actually. But I send my very best regards."

Myrtle shot him a look and then asked Martin for his sister's address so they could bring her food, as well.

Chapter Eight

As they walked toward the car, Myrtle said, "You're entirely too modest. You were there when I made the casserole, after all. You could take some credit for it, if you'd wanted."

Miles shook his head violently. "No. I never take credit when credit isn't warranted."

"How pedantic of you, Miles!" said Myrtle a bit crossly. They climbed into the car and Myrtle looked down at the floorboard to see the other casserole. "Let's take this over to Annie right away, since it's not on ice. Maybe we should have brought a cooler."

Miles said, "We weren't in Martin's house long enough to create a problem, I don't think." But he did drive a little faster over to Annie's house.

He asked, "What does Annie do?"

Myrtle said, "She's a teacher. She and I have talked about it before, actually. I don't think she's as crazy about teaching as she thought she'd be. That's probably one of the reasons she was interested in moving away from town and starting over."

Miles said, "I thought teaching was sort of like preaching—you needed to have some sort of calling to do it. It's not something suited to everyone."

"She might have simply been determined to do something completely different from what her mother wanted her to do," said Myrtle with a shrug. "Lillian was pestering Annie to go into the flower business with her and there Annie was getting a teaching certificate. It must have driven Lillian nuts. Which was precisely what Annie wanted, I bet."

They drove up to a much more modest home than Martin's had been. It was a small duplex apartment with overgrown landscaping.

Myrtle rang the doorbell. There was a flutter of the curtains near the front door and then Annie peered out. She had sharp features, bright red hair and a suspicious expression on her face that quickly turned to surprise when she spotted Myrtle. She unlocked the front door.

"Miss Myrtle!" said Annie, opening the door wide. "What a surprise to see you!"

"Yes, dear. I was so sorry to hear the news about your poor mama." Myrtle thrust the casserole at her. The casserole, having sat in a hot vehicle during the visit with Martin, was decidedly fishy in aroma and Annie's nose crinkled just a little bit. Miles made an odd noise, which he quickly covered with coughing.

Myrtle gave Miles a reproving look. "And this is Miles Bradford. Perhaps you've seen him around town."

Miles gave Annie an apologetic smile to cover either the casserole, the intrusion, or both. "I knew your mother. I'm very sorry."

Annie said, "Please come in. Just forgive the mess—yesterday was such a long day and I haven't had the chance to clean up."

"Don't even think about it," said Myrtle, following Annie in. Although it was tough, as Myrtle quickly glanced around the small living room for a place to sit, *not* to think about it. Annie had papers and boxes and things all over the room. Miles patted his pockets for the comforting feel of the hand sanitizer bottle as Annie whisked the aromatic casserole away to the kitchen.

Miles gave Myrtle a silent, questioning look and Myrtle hissed, "Just uncover a chair, Miles! It isn't rocket science."

Miles looked miserably at the sofa, which would require extreme excavation. "I hate to move her things."

"It's not as if her things are *organized*. I don't think we're messing up some sort of arcane system." Myrtle picked up a pile of clothing and papers from an armchair and dropped them on the floor.

Annie came back into the room and flushed. "I'm so sorry about this. I promise I'm not usually so much of a slob. I'm kind of stuck in a transition and don't know what to do. The more I stew over it, the less-inclined I am to try to make sense out of this room."

Myrtle gave her a sympathetic look. "That sounds awful. What sort of transition are you struggling with?"

Annie sighed. "You probably know from Mama that I was planning on leaving Bradley. She told everyone about it because she was so unhappy I wasn't going to take over the flower shop."

Myrtle said, "Not everyone has an interest in flowers, my dear. Or a green thumb. I'm sure Lillian would have understood on some level, even if she was disappointed."

Annie smiled at her. "You're nice to try to make me feel better. The truth was, Miss Myrtle, Mama was a total harridan." Her face grew darkly reflective. "I never could do anything right. No matter what course I took, she was forever scolding me. I have the feeling that even if I *had* decided to work at the flower shop she'd have been telling me all the things I was doing wrong . . . selecting the wrong flowers, putting them in the wrong vase, arranging them wrong. It wouldn't have been any better."

"And she wasn't pleased with your decision to go into teaching, I know," said Myrtle sadly.

Annie sighed. "That's putting it mildly. She was furious and stopped giving me financial assistance for school. Mama told me I'd be an awful teacher and I'd be miserable. The horrible thing is she might have been right. You've been great to listen to me talk about school, Miss Myrtle. But the fact of the matter is, I'm worried I'm never really going to get the hang of teaching. That it won't get better with time."

Miles cleared his throat and said, "It must be a difficult occupation to settle into."

Annie gave him a grateful look. "It is. Right now, there haven't been as many good days as there've been bad days and I'm just concerned it won't get any better." She gave a short laugh. "That's sort of my explanation about why my house looks like this. I started packing my things a couple of weeks ago, thinking I'd try to take a teaching position in another town and get away from my family. But then I worried about starting over somewhere else, struggling with teaching and without any friends or community support." She shrugged.

Myrtle said, "You wanted to escape your family? Is Martin not very helpful, either?"

Annie snorted. "Martin is concerned with one thing and one thing only: Martin. He's incredibly obnoxious and a chronic liar. Plus, it drove me crazy to see him kissing up to Mama all the time."

Myrtle and Miles glanced at each other. Myrtle said, "We actually ran by Martin's house on the way here and delivered some food."

Annie said, "Then you saw the mansion on the lake. Martin is a ridiculous show-off. And yet he and Mama always got along better than she and I did. I had to sit and endure family dinners together where Martin acted all sweet and Mama ate it up. Then she'd either barely acknowledge me or would spend the evening telling me how I always screwed everything up."

Myrtle said slowly, "That sounds like a terrible situation to have to deal with. I can understand you thinking about moving."

"Most of the time I wanted to get as far away as I possibly could. I started applying for teaching positions and I've had a few offers for other towns in the state. That's one nice thing about being a teacher: you can find a job anywhere," said Annie. She shook her head. "But then, when I heard the news yesterday, I wasn't sure what to do anymore. And I've been changing my mind about moving every minute anyway." She gave a short laugh. "When Mama died, I was apparently watching a recording of my guilty pleasure show . . . *Tomorrow's Promise*."

Myrtle said, "Oh, that's Miles's and my show!"

Miles gave her a dark look. He didn't like her to spread that tidbit of information around.

"Back to Martin, though. I apologize for anything that happened while you were there," said Annie. "Did he try and sell you insurance?"

Myrtle said, "Not very hard."

Miles snorted.

Annie rolled her eyes. "But he did try. That's just par for the course for Martin. I can't figure what I've done to deserve such a dysfunctional family."

Myrtle said, "At least yours can't be as bad as Simon and Josephine's."

Annie gazed blankly at Myrtle.

Myrtle said, "Remember from the show? Simon accidentally married his half-sister?"

Miles gave Myrtle a curious look.

"Oh! Oh, of course. Sorry, I drew a blank there. I tried to sleep last night but clearly I didn't get as much as I should have," said Annie.

Myrtle said, "Maybe you can catch up on sleep tonight. Or have a nap? Maybe after eating the casserole and having a full tummy, you'll be able to sleep a little better."

Miles shuddered.

Myrtle said, "And of course we'll all sleep better when the police finally arrest whoever is responsible for your mother's death. If we only had some idea who might be behind it!" She looked expectantly at Annie.

Annie tilted her head to one side in thought. "Mama didn't get along with many people well, but there was one person in particular she was really tough on. I'll tell you what I told Red, Miss Myrtle—I'd talk to Bianca Lloyd."

Myrtle frowned. "Bianca Lloyd. The name doesn't seem to ring a bell for me."

"She works at the flower shop." Annie snorted. "She's the one person Mama was ruder to than me. The way Mama talked to Bianca was scandalous. She thought Bianca was just as hopeless as I was. She didn't like Bianca's arrangements, her choice of flowers, the way she dressed, anything. Mama was practically abusive to her."

Miles asked, "Would she have come by your mother's house?"

Annie shrugged. "I have no idea. I tried to be involved as little as possible in Mama's affairs. Who knows?"

Myrtle asked, "Do you know what's going to happen with Lillian's shop?"

Annie made a face. "Not yet. Martin and I are supposed to meet with Mama's lawyer sometime today. That should be a fun meeting. But I know one thing—I don't want anything to do with that shop. When I think about the shop, I think about Mama. When I think about Mama, I don't feel good about myself . . . that's the kind of effect she had on me."

Myrtle said, "But surely you should at least benefit if the shop is sold."

"I don't really want a penny of that money. It would be tainted because it came from the shop."

Myrtle nodded. "I can certainly understand where you're coming from. And now I think we should let you be. Thanks so much for inviting us in, Annie."

A few minutes later, Myrtle and Miles were back in the car.

"Where are we heading?" asked Miles.

"Oh, I think a trip to the grocery store is probably in order. After breakfast this morning, I think I've depleted most of my stock pantry and fridge items."

Miles set off in the direction of downtown Bradley and the Piggly-Wiggly grocery store.

Miles said, "That was something."

"Yes, wasn't it? That poor girl. It sounds like Lillian really tried to destroy her self-esteem, doesn't it?"

Miles said, "I meant more of the mess in there."

Myrtle rolled her eyes. "For heaven's sake, Miles. Annie's life is clearly in turmoil and that turmoil is being expressed through the disorder in her house."

"When *I* feel turmoil, I usually like to straighten things up," said Miles. "But yes, I totally agree Lillian was poisonous for Annie if what Annie says is true." He glanced at Myrtle. "I really didn't know Lillian all that well. Was she like that with other people? Critical, I mean?"

Myrtle said, "Well, she certainly wasn't critical around me. I'd have put her right in her place. But yes. She was also a woman who knew her own mind."

"It's odd she and Erma would be friends," said Miles.

"It's odd *anybody* would be friends with Erma."

Miles said, "But Lillian sounds as if she was such a perfectionist and so precise and critical. And then Erma is . . . Erma."

Myrtle said, "One thing they had in common was the fact they loved complaining about their health issues. Apparently, Lillian had as many of them as Erma does. Besides, I'm not at all convinced Erma and Lillian were as close as Erma professes. But think of it this way—Lillian could easily push Erma around. And Lillian liked nothing better than to push people around. We'd be at garden club meetings and discussing an upcoming meeting or event and Lillian would be very scornful of any ideas other than whatever she proposed."

"How did the rest of the club respond to *that*?" asked Miles as he carefully navigated the car down the street.

"In various ways. Some of the women became defensive. Others figured that, since Lillian was the resident flower expert, they should defer to her. And others, like me, simply didn't care enough to have an opinion."

Miles said, "Not having an opinion doesn't sound like you."

Myrtle said, "I only express opinions when I'm passionate about something. Who could be passionate about garden club?"

"Tippy."

"*Besides* Tippy. Anyway, I think Tippy is a fanatic only because she likes to do everything perfectly." Myrtle frowned. "That reminds me, I need to call her. She's probably on pins and needles worrying about whether we should continue holding that wretched auction."

As Miles pulled in front of the grocery store and parked, Myrtle pulled out her phone. "I'll stay in the car while I chat with her. I do hate seeing other people in the grocery store talking loudly on their phones."

Miles looked as if he'd rather Myrtle attempt multitasking by shopping and chatting at the same time, but obligingly waited.

"Tippy? It's Myrtle. Listen, I spoke with Martin and he said we should continue on with the auction . . . he didn't think it was inappropriate at all."

Tippy breathed a sigh of relief but then asked sharply, "And Annie? Have you spoken with her?"

Myrtle made a face at Miles. She'd forgotten to bring it up. "I didn't, Tippy, but I can tell you Annie is not exactly bereaved. She doesn't even want anything to do with the shop, just because Lillian owned it. I know she won't think us insensitive for proceeding with the auction."

"Well, that is a relief! I've been worried sick because of all the deposits we've already made to the caterer and whatnot. Which reminds me, I need to speak with Lillian's assistant at the flower shop to make sure she's still able to supply the flowers for the auction, even without Lillian's help," said Tippy.

Myrtle quickly said, "I'm happy to take care of that, Tippy. Miles and I were going to go by the flower shop this afternoon."

Miles rolled his eyes.

"Really?" asked Tippy doubtfully. "Were you? That would be great, if you're sure."

"I couldn't be surer. I'll talk to you later, Tippy, I'm at the store. Bye-bye." Myrtle hung up and opened the car door. Miles glumly followed.

"We were going to the flower shop?" he asked in a pointed voice.

"Well, we *could* have been going to the flower shop, as far as Tippy knows. Maybe it's Elaine's birthday. Maybe I wanted to get an arrangement of flowers for the church sanctuary to honor someone's memory."

Miles rolled his eyes. "Because you donate arrangements at the church all the time."

"Well I *could*. Anyway, Tippy was happy to have us go over there and now we have a reason to speak with that Bianca woman Annie was talking about."

Miles pulled out a grocery cart and he and Myrtle proceeded down the aisles.

"What do you need?" he asked.

"Everything," said Myrtle. "I can't for the life of me figure out what Red and I purchased during our last shopping trip. I don't have much of anything in the house right now unless I want to make a meal of pickles and olives." She tilted her head thoughtfully. "Actually, the olives might have made a nice touch for the casseroles I made for Martin and Annie. Pity I didn't think of them."

Miles gazed briefly upwards, bearing a thankful expression.

Myrtle tossed a few cans of soup into her cart and then stared down the aisle. She hissed at Miles, "That's Lillian's neighbor, isn't it? The one Erma was talking to?"

Chapter Nine

Miles peered down the aisle. "I suppose so. She sort of looks like her, anyway."

"Martin said his mother had some sort of falling out with Tallulah, remember? We should talk to her."

Miles winced. "We're accosting suspects in the grocery store now?"

"We have to make our opportunities where we can find them! Seize the day and all that," said Myrtle firmly. She walked with determination toward the woman with Miles reluctantly trailing behind with the grocery cart.

When the woman spotted Myrtle, she lit up and hurried toward her with just as much determination.

"You were at Lillian's house yesterday morning, weren't you?" the woman asked.

"Yes. I'm Myrtle Clover and this is my friend, Miles Bradford. You were Lillian's neighbor, is that right?"

The woman nodded. "Yes, I was. Such a terrible tragedy." But her eyes were gleaming. "I'm Tallulah Porter. Lillian right lived next-door to me."

Myrtle said, "A tragedy, for sure. Was Lillian a good neighbor? I know her yard was very nice, at least. I have a neighbor who does *not* keep her yard up and it's a constant aggravation. It would be lovely to have a neighbor with a green thumb, like Lillian."

Tallulah tilted her head doubtfully. "I *suppose* you could say she had a green thumb. But it wasn't like she was a farmer or owned a garden center or anything. She arranged flowers—that didn't mean she grew them. But I guess she did all right with her yard. She was kind of funny about it. Real particular."

She turned her attention to Miles and he shifted away slightly. "From what I hear, you found Lillian. Is that right?"

Miles said stiffly, "Unfortunately. It was a terrible day. Mostly for Lillian."

Tallulah looked disappointed that Miles didn't appear open to sharing gory details.

Myrtle asked, "You must have known Lillian pretty well, being such a close neighbor."

Tallulah looked pleased to be the resident expert on a murder victim. "In some ways. Like I said, she was real particular about things. I've seen her outside many a day with a pair of scissors clipping any grass blades the yard man had missed."

Myrtle said wryly, "It's a good thing she didn't have *my* yard man, Dusty. She'd have been out there for hours."

Miles said, "Was Lillian a difficult neighbor to have? I always think it's hard when one has a difficult neighbor." He cut his eyes sideways at Myrtle and Myrtle glowered at him.

Tallulah pursed her lips. "I don't know that I'd say she was *always* difficult. We did have a slight squabble between us . . .

nothing important, you understand. I got 'Yard of the Month' from the neighborhood association and Lillian was *very* upset." Tallulah smiled faintly at the memory.

"You must keep a very nice yard, yourself," said Myrtle. She reflected darkly on Dusty again.

"I have a nice collection of roses and daylilies," said Tallulah. "I think Lillian envied them, I really do. I'm not going to say Lillian *didn't* have a nice yard. But the truth is that she spent a lot of time at work and that didn't leave a lot of extra time for her to tinker with her plants. As for me, I was left enough money from my husband when he died to keep me comfortable. And then only thing I have to distract me from my yard is golf."

"You're a golfer?" asked Myrtle. Somehow, Tallulah didn't seem to match Myrtle's vision of a golfer. However, she figured her vision of a golfer was hopelessly outdated since it involved pudgy old men in loud clothing. Or Crazy Dan with his very own version of the classic sport.

"Yes," said Tallulah, puffing up with pride. "I've even won regional competitions. I have trophies at home."

Myrtle quickly continued, hoping to cut Tallulah off before she and Miles received any unwanted invitations to view the trophies. To butter Tallulah up again, she said, "I'm sure the police must have been very interested in asking you questions. After all, being right next door, you might have seen or heard something. Or were you out of the house when Lillian died?"

Tallulah looked smug. "They *did* ask a lot of questions, yes, because I was at home the whole time. I noticed they asked a lot about the kind of person Lillian was. They wanted to get a better picture of her."

Miles asked, "And what did you say about her?"

"That Lillian could be very challenging to be around. I could hear her yell at all kinds of people who've come to work at Lillian's house: painters, landscapers, even the poor guy who came out to pressure-wash her driveway and front walk."

Myrtle said, "Did they ask you if you'd seen or heard anything suspicious?"

Tallulah looked uncomfortable for a moment before saying, "They did, but I didn't hear a thing. Whoever did this must have been very quiet."

Myrtle couldn't imagine that smashing a dog feeding station over someone's head could have been all that quiet. But she didn't push it. "Do you have an opinion over who might have killed Lillian?"

Here Tallulah's face lit up again. "I sure do, and I shared it with the cops, too. They wrote down every word in their notebooks. Annie. That daughter of hers must have done it. If *I'd* been Annie, I'd have wanted to get rid of Lillian, too. Lillian did nothing but berate her for years and years. The girl is in her mid or late twenties now and I've never seen an unhappier child. She should be having the time of her life at this point and instead she's been stuck here in Bradley getting yelled at by her mother all the time. Ridiculous."

Tallulah leaned in, her face the picture of ghoulish enjoyment. "Do you think the police will be arresting Annie today? Because of what I told them?"

Myrtle gave Tallulah an annoyed look. "The police can't simply arrest someone because someone else said she was yelled at. They have to have evidence the person perpetrated the crime."

Tallulah's face fell. "I suppose so. Well, maybe they'll find it in the house. Did you see anything that looked like evidence?" Tallulah turned her avid expression to Miles.

Miles's eyes narrowed. "Looking for evidence wasn't exactly my focus. I wanted to see if Lillian was all right first. Then I wanted to call the police. And leave."

Tallulah looked disappointed.

Miles glanced at his watch in a pointed way. "Myrtle, shouldn't we finish up your shopping?"

Myrtle said, "Yes. Yes, we should get on with things. Good speaking with you, Tallulah."

As soon as they moved out of earshot, Miles said, "Good speaking with her?"

"Well, I couldn't very well say it was good to escape from her, could I? I know Lillian wasn't the easiest person to get along with, but I'll bet my bottom dollar Tallulah wasn't exactly the perfect neighbor, either. I have the feeling there were bad feelings between the two of them," said Myrtle.

Miles stopped the cart as Myrtle distractedly threw in a bunch of dairy products. "Tallulah herself said there were bad feelings between them. The 'Yard of the Month' award that Tallulah won."

Myrtle said, "I bet there was a lot more than just a silly award behind their bad feelings." She frowned at the grocery store aisles. "Now I'm thrown all off-course. Maybe I should just do a longer grocery store visit when I've had the chance to make out a thoughtful list. And when I have my coupons with me."

Miles looked in her cart. "Do you even have the right ingredients to make something for supper?"

Myrtle scowled into her cart. "I could eat a can of soup."

Miles grabbed some eggs off the shelf. "Here. Now you can at least have scrambled eggs." He dodged down a nearby aisle and came back holding a box. "And here's granola cereal. Combined with your milk, you should be set for breakfast."

"Good enough since I'm not particular. Let's check out and run this stuff by my house. Then we can head over to the flower shop and run Tippy's errand. And pelt Bianca with questions, of course," added Myrtle.

Forty-five minutes later, they'd dumped off Myrtle's groceries and were pulling up to the flower shop.

Miles sat in the car for a moment after turning off the engine.

Myrtle said, "Come on, Miles, for heaven's sake."

"This won't take long, will it? My lack of sleep is starting to catch up with me." He blinked a few times.

Myrtle's eyes narrowed. "Okay, that's it. I'm driving on the way back."

"That's really not necessary," said Miles quickly.

"Yes, it is. It's either that or I'm walking back home. I'm not putting myself in the situation of being in a vehicle with someone who's going to fall asleep at the wheel."

Miles muttered, "If you walked, you'd likely make it back home at the same time as if you'd driven."

Myrtle glared at him. "I don't drive that slowly!"

Miles briefly closed his eyes. "Let's just make this flower shop visit as fast as possible."

The shop was not exactly a cute shop. Myrtle said, "This shop is just like Lillian. All business. When I picture a flower shop, I'm thinking about ivy climbing up the sides and red trim and adorable arrangements in sweet little pots outside."

"That's definitely not the vibe I'm getting from this place," agreed Miles.

They walked in and instead of a bell ringing, there was an electronic beep that reminded Myrtle of the class bells from her school teaching days. A mousy middle-aged woman of about forty jumped as she heard it as if conditioned to bad experiences when the beep blared. Her red hair was pulled back in a messy ponytail and her clothing was bright but didn't match.

She stopped her half-hearted messing with a potted plant and hurried toward them. "Can I help you?" she asked anxiously.

Myrtle said, "I'm Myrtle Clover and this is my friend Miles Bradford. We're members of the garden club that's holding the silent auction."

Now the red-haired woman looked even more concerned. "I'm Bianca Lloyd. Oh dear. Is everything all right?"

"Yes, it's all fine. We checked in with the family and they said the club should continue with the auction, even under the circumstances," said Myrtle.

Bianca paled slightly when Myrtle mentioned the *circumstances* and looked down at the floor. "I see. I was wondering what would happen to the auction with Lillian being gone."

Myrtle said, "We're just checking in to make sure the arrangements for the auction will remain on time. I have the feeling Lillian herself was probably planning on putting them together, considering she was a garden club member."

Now Bianca looked even more worried. "Yeees, she was. Oh dear. She didn't even tell me what she'd planned for the event. Sometimes, if she was handling something herself, she didn't fill me in."

Miles cleared his throat. "Perhaps she had notes you could find? Sketches? That type of thing?"

Bianca's eyes filled with tears. "Nothing like that, no. Lillian always took a lot of pride in the fact she was able to plan arrangements in her head. I have no idea what she wanted to do."

Myrtle was alarmed about the tears and said briskly, "No worries. Just come up with whatever you think is best. We won't know the difference since we didn't know what Lillian was planning."

Bianca gave her a relieved look and hastily rubbed her eyes with the back of her hand, resulting in a rather muddy smear across her face from whatever she was working with before they came in.

"Oh, thank you," she breathed. "Thank you. I was about to be in a total panic. I know Lillian was *so particular* about her events. I hate to think what she'd have said about whatever I put together."

Myrtle said, "It doesn't *really* matter, does it? Whatever you come up with will make the venue look better than it ordinarily does and that's the whole point." She paused. "Was Lillian always such an impossible person to work for?"

Bianca's eyes grew huge. "I was so grateful to Lillian. My husband divorced me five years ago and I didn't know what I was going to do. I'd been an at-home Mama with Tim and wasn't qualified to do anything at all. I mean, the last job I had was working as a sales clerk in the dress department of the mall. But no one was hiring for retail and my ex-husband wasn't sending me any money at all. No child support even."

Myrtle gave a ferocious frown. "He's not allowed to get away with that. The courts would make him pay."

Bianca's thin shoulders gave a half-hearted shrug. "I didn't have money to take him to court to force him to. Anyway, there I was with no real skills and no income and a child to feed. And Lillian took me in."

Myrtle said, "It must have been quite a terrible shock to hear the news about Lillian."

Bianca nodded. "Yes. I couldn't really wrap my head around it when the police told me. Lillian seemed like too strong of a woman to ever die." She gave a short laugh. "I know that sounds ridiculous, but that's the way I felt. And I'd had such a quiet last day and morning leading up to it. The night before, I helped Tim with his homework until it was time to go to bed. When he was at school yesterday morning, I came over to the shop to get started early on the arrangements before customers started coming in."

Myrtle said, "So you didn't run by Lillian's house yesterday morning? I'd wondered if maybe you had to sometimes stop by for work."

Bianca blinked at her. "I've never been to Lillian's house. She was a very private woman and wouldn't have liked me being over there." She gave a shudder as if envisioning exactly how irritated Lillian would have been at such an intrusion into her private life. "The only time she ever even spoke about something personal was when she'd tell me about her health problems sometimes. I wondered if maybe they put her in a bad mood. You know, when she wasn't feeling well."

There was a sound in the back of the shop and Bianca jumped and whirled around. "Excuse me for a minute," she murmured and hurried to the back room.

Chapter Ten

Myrtle and Miles glanced at each other as they heard Bianca say, "Are you all right? Everything okay? Do you need some more water?"

A few minutes later, she came back with an apologetic expression on her face. "I'm so sorry about that. My son wasn't feeling well this morning so I couldn't take him to school. But I didn't want to not show up at work, especially with everything going on."

Miles asked, "He's sick?" He patted his pockets absently and pulled out his hand sanitizer.

Bianca said quickly, "It's his stomach—just a little virus or something. I brought an air mattress from home for him to sleep on. I figured with some sleep, he'd be better soon."

Myrtle said, "Back to Lillian's death, Bianca. Miles and I were most upset about it, naturally, and have been talking about who could have done such a dreadful thing."

"Did you come to any conclusions?" asked Bianca. She blinked anxiously. "It's terrible to think a murderer is running around Bradley. I have Tim to think about."

"Sadly, we *didn't* come to any conclusions. But we'd like to know what you think, since you spent so much time with Lillian. Was there any trouble in her life? Anything you can think of that might somehow have led to her death?" asked Myrtle.

Bianca looked uncomfortable. "Well, I don't know if anything I've seen has anything to do with Lillian's murder. I'd hate for somebody to get into trouble for something they didn't do."

"Oh, we're just talking," said Myrtle airily. "It's not as if Miles and I are with the police."

Miles carefully applied another layer of hand sanitizer and gave Bianca a reassuring smile.

Bianca took a deep breath. "All right. I guess the only thing I can think of is the argument Lillian had with her son." She quickly added, "Like I said, I'm sure it doesn't mean anything. Families have fights all the time."

Myrtle nodded. "What sort of argument was it?"

Bianca said, "Martin had apparently been trying to reach Lillian all day at the shop. She and I were working on arrangements for a big wedding and reception for the next day and we were slammed. Her phone would ring and Lillian would stop what she was doing and glance at it. Then she'd give a huge sigh and ignore it. Finally, she wouldn't even look at it anymore when it rang, just let it go to voice mail."

Myrtle said, "How did you know it was Martin? Did Lillian tell you that?"

Bianca said, "Oh, no. No, like I said, Lillian wanted to keep her private life private. But after a while, Martin came into the shop. Usually he was so charming, but this time he was really angry. He yelled at Lillian for not picking up his phone calls."

Miles raised his eyebrows. "I'm guessing Lillian didn't like being yelled at."

Bianca gave him a small smile. "You're right. She snapped right back at him that she was very busy and didn't have time for his nonsense."

Miles said, "Did he say anything about why he'd called?"

Bianca looked uncomfortable. "Something to do about money. I was so embarrassed at that point that I wanted to crawl into a hole. Like I said, Lillian was very private and she wouldn't have wanted to have a conversation like that in front of me. But there we were, working on this important order for a wedding and I figured Lillian wouldn't be happy if I took a break or something, either."

Myrtle tilted her head thoughtfully. "Money. What about money?"

Bianca made a face. "I guess Martin wanted some. For some kind of reason. Anyway, Lillian wouldn't even continue having the conversation with him and he eventually stormed out."

"I'd heard they had a good relationship," mused Myrtle.

"Oh, I think they *did*. Most of the time, anyway. But even in the best families, you have arguments, right? This was totally out of the ordinary, as far as I could tell, anyway. Usually when Martin came in, Lillian lit up from inside. Actually, I was always glad when Martin came by the shop because it usually put Lillian in such a good mood," said Bianca.

Miles asked, "Did he come by the shop very often?"

"Regularly. Maybe once or twice a week? He sometimes came with little presents for Lillian, too, like a bottle of wine he thought she'd like or an old family photo he'd had framed.

She loved it when he did that kind of thing." Bianca's face held a wistful expression as if she wished someone would do something like that for her.

Miles said, "Did her daughter come by the store some, too?"

Bianca gave him a wry look. "As little as she could possibly get away with. Annie didn't seem at all interested in the shop. But every time Annie pulled away from Lillian and the shop, Lillian got more determined to get her involved in it." She flushed. "I'm sorry, I really shouldn't be talking about the family like this."

Myrtle said briskly, "You're just helping us get a picture of what might have happened to Lillian."

Bianca's eyebrows shot up in alarm. "I don't want to give you the impression that Martin or Annie might have killed their Mama. That's not what I meant at all. I was just talking about how their relationships were."

"Who *do* you think might have killed Lillian, then?" asked Myrtle.

Bianca swallowed nervously. "I don't have any idea. I don't want to throw blame at anybody because I don't know—I was at home with Tim when this all happened."

Myrtle gave her one of her old school teacher looks. "Don't be silly, Bianca, no one is saying you're supplying evidence here. We're merely talking among ourselves."

Bianca relaxed a little.

"Was there anyone besides family that Lillian had any run-ins with? Any incidents?" asked Myrtle.

Bianca said slowly, "Well, she did have some issues with Rowan Blaine."

Myrtle looked pensive. "Rowan Blaine. He's the caterer, isn't he?"

Miles raised his eyebrows. "*The* caterer?"

"It's only a small town, Miles. He's the only one who's local. You have to go to another town to find anyone else," said Myrtle.

Bianca said, "That's right. They spent a lot of time together because they work the same types of events: anniversaries, weddings, wakes, parties. They were around each other a lot and I guess their personalities really didn't mesh."

"Do you have any examples?" asked Myrtle.

Bianca quickly shook her head. "Oh no. No, it's just an observation of mine. It's not anything major, just some professional rivalry or something." She looked anxiously at the wall clock. "I'm sorry to have to do this, but I really should get back to work. Especially since I need to figure out what Lillian wanted to do for the silent auction arrangements. And I probably need to check in on Tim again and make sure he's all right." She cast a glance toward the back room of the shop.

"Of course," said Myrtle smoothly. "We'll let you get back to it."

A minute later, Myrtle and Miles climbed into his car.

Miles said, "There seem to be plenty of people who didn't care for Lillian very much."

"Indeed. I'm rather surprised Rowan Blaine was one of them. He always seems so congenial."

Miles started off down the street. "Bianca said it was professional rivalry."

"Yes, but that doesn't even make *sense*. They weren't in the same profession together," said Myrtle crossly.

"Maybe they simply annoyed each other on the occasions where their paths crossed," said Miles with a shrug.

Myrtle rummaged around in her large purse until she found her phone. "I suppose. Maybe they were both Type A people. I'm going to call Tippy and report in on the flowers. Then I'm going to see if she needs me to follow up on the catering. That would be our best bet for talking to Rowan."

Miles's face fell. "Not today, Myrtle. Set it up for tomorrow. I can't do anything else today without getting sleep first."

"You did really well with Bianca," said Myrtle.

"I rallied. Briefly. But now I need to go home and put my feet up."

Myrtle gave a gusty sigh and called Tippy. It ended up that Tippy's husband was having to have emergency dental work done and needed a driver. The next day, she had her own appointments and was delighted for Myrtle to take on the caterer for the auction.

Miles pulled up into Myrtle's driveway, his expression relieved. "All right, then. See you tomorrow."

Myrtle looked at her watch. "Make sure you don't turn in *too* early or you'll end up waking up in the middle of the night and not being able to go back to sleep."

Miles shook his head. "There is absolutely no chance of that."

At three a.m., there was a tap on Myrtle's front door. She smiled to herself and opened the front door. Miles was standing there, already fully dressed in khaki pants and a button-down shirt as if it were much later in the day.

"Come on in and have some coffee," said Myrtle. She was still wearing her long bathrobe and slippers. "Did you see the newspaper outside, yet?"

Miles shook his head. "I believe three o'clock is a bit early for the paper to arrive." He gave her a look through narrowed eyes. "You must have somehow cursed me yesterday when you said I'd wake up in the middle of the night."

Myrtle gave a shrug as she grabbed a mug for Miles. "It's common sense. If you go to bed at six p.m., it's unlikely you're going to sleep through the entire night. Just try again tonight a little later. Maybe nine o'clock."

Miles sleepily sat down at the kitchen table, stifling a yawn with one hand.

"Here, you can help me with the crossword puzzle," said Myrtle, shoving a newspaper at him.

Miles quirked an eyebrow. "You don't *need* help with the crossword puzzle. Besides, this is yesterday's paper. I've already worked the puzzle and know all the answers. Because I didn't sleep."

"I didn't have time to finish it yesterday. It was something of a busy day. Anyway, it bothers me when it's not completed."

Miles obediently picked up a pencil and started filling in the answers.

After that, they watched Myrtle's tape of *Tomorrow's Promise*. Miles was mostly awake although he fell asleep during John and Marsha's wedding scene, which annoyed Myrtle, who wanted to talk about the wedding.

Myrtle loudly coughed and Miles jerked in his seat and blinked several times.

"I think hats at weddings are odd, don't you?" asked Myrtle. "It's like they're trying to look British. When Americans attempt to look British, it's impossible for them to pull it off."

Miles nodded blearily, squinting at the television. "I suppose so. I thought John and Marsha were already married."

"They *were* married, but they've been divorced for several seasons, remember?"

Miles shook his head. "But they've been having romantic assignations."

"Yes, but secretly, because they're both dating other people. John was dating Samantha and Marsha was dating Sebastian," said Myrtle.

Miles blinked again at the television. "And now they're getting married again."

"Yes, because they worked through their problems. Remember? They divorced because Marsha thought John was being secretive because he was having an affair. But actually, he was being secretive because he had a terminal cancer diagnosis and didn't want to break Marsha's heart."

Miles frowned. "So he broke her heart by divorcing her, instead."

"But his *intentions* were good," said Myrtle. "Really, Miles, I don't understand how you could have forgotten all this."

"I think it's coming back to me," said Miles slowly. "And John's cancer diagnosis was wrong. The doctor was disbarred."

"No, that was *Amelie's* cancer diagnosis that was wrong. But John's cancer was miraculously cured when he went through those experimental treatments up north. Then he was able to tell Marsha everything," said Myrtle.

"I can't keep up," muttered Miles.

Myrtle said, "What really bothers me is Annie using our soap opera as an alibi when clearly she had no idea what was going on with the show whatsoever."

"Maybe you should tell Red that. We know *he* certainly doesn't watch *Tomorrow's Promise*."

Myrtle said defiantly, "I'm definitely not going to offer Red Clover any information unless he comes to me and asks about it. After all, I'm the resident expert on that soap opera. He should be coming over here and begging me to tell him if Annie has actually been watching the show or is lying through her teeth."

"Somehow I don't see Red doing that," said Miles.

"Well then, let him watch it himself and figure out Annie isn't telling the truth," said Myrtle.

"Annie probably just came up with the first alibi she could think of," said Miles with a shrug. "It might not really mean anything. She knows she has a good motive for her mother's death. Everyone in town apparently knows Lillian was incredibly demanding and rude to Annie. Maybe she panicked when Red started asking her questions and latched onto the show."

Myrtle shrugged. "Then she should have read a recap of the show online before she started talking about it with us. But I agree with you—Annie certainly has motive. After all, she was wanting to leave Bradley altogether in order to escape her mother."

"Although Annie seemed to think Bianca could be angry enough to kill her mother," said Miles. He was looking slightly more awake now that his brain was getting a bit of a workout.

Myrtle said, "Which was a good way to deflect attention from her."

"I have to say that I thought Bianca would be . . . different."

Myrtle said, "You came up with an opinion on her before you saw her?"

"Sort of. I thought she would be a little like Annie, I guess. Or maybe sort of defensive. The kind of person who's been yelled at for years and is tired of it," said Miles.

"But Bianca acted as if she was grateful to Lillian for giving her a job just when she needed it the most. That her no-good husband had left her with a child and no money and Lillian stepped in and helped her out."

Miles said, "Maybe she was just trying to hang onto a job."

"Maybe so," said Myrtle. "Then there's Martin. He is clearly not exactly what he seems."

Miles made a face. "He seems like an insurance salesman to me. And a rather aggressive one."

Myrtle waved her hand impatiently. "Yes, but that's not important. I'm immune, as I mentioned. No, I think he's hiding something else. That argument with his mother sounds as if it might have been interesting, especially since he's painting this picture of himself as the adoring and beloved son."

Miles said, "At any rate, it doesn't sound like he was on the receiving end of the same treatment Annie was getting from Lillian."

"And then there's Tallulah. She's really something else. I think she and Lillian had a lot of the same personality traits—and they weren't good ones, either. I'm sure she's not telling the whole truth about why she and Lillian were at odds."

Miles said, "You don't think it was Yard of the Month?"

"I certainly don't. And now we have Rowan Blaine as a potential suspect. It seems as though half the people in town didn't like Lillian," said Myrtle. "Wanda was right about her being in danger. Too bad Lillian was too snooty to listen to me."

Miles said slowly, "I'm beginning to think I made a terrible mistake in joining garden club. Especially if Lillian was a typical garden club member."

Myrtle said, "I told you to develop your ability to say no. Now you're in all sorts of organizations."

"I don't really mind the Scrabble club anymore," said Miles thoughtfully. "It's mostly just garden club."

"Maybe after this silent auction is over and you're done with the heavy lifting, you can simply tell Tippy you didn't realize when you signed up that you wouldn't be able to contribute enough time to the club," said Myrtle.

Miles sighed. "What activity is it that's supposed to be taking up so much of my time? Watching soap operas? Doing crosswords? Having coffee with you?"

"None of her business. Besides, Tippy is too much of a lady to ask you. She'll tell you not to worry and cross you off the membership list," said Myrtle. She looked at her watch. "How could it possibly still be this early in the morning? I thought surely it was time to run over and see Rowan."

"It's still dark outside," said Miles with a yawn. He glanced at the clock. "Now that I've had coffee, I'm suddenly feeling very tired."

"Which makes very little sense, Miles."

"I know. Still, I'm going to go home and put my feet up for a while and see if I'm able to catch a few winks. Will you call me when you're ready to see Rowan?"

"His office apparently opens at eight, so I'll call you around 7:30," said Myrtle.

Miles frowned. "I don't think it will take thirty minutes to get there. More like seven."

"Yes, but you may want to eat something or brush your hair or your teeth. Rowan is very proper. He may not appreciate growling stomachs or messy hair or food stuck in teeth," said Myrtle.

Miles looked alarmed. "Do I have those things?" He abruptly stood up and walked to a mirror in Myrtle's living room, gazing anxiously at himself.

"Not right now, but who knows what you may look like later? After all, you haven't had any sleep and you might do any number of random and peculiar things," said Myrtle.

Chapter Eleven

But when Myrtle called Miles at 7:30, he'd clearly been up for quite some time. Perhaps the specter of appearing uncouth had been hanging over him. At any rate, he seemed in tiptop shape when he picked Myrtle up to head to Rowan's office a bit later.

Rowan had a cute brick office in downtown Bradley that had once been a house. It looked more like it was a flower shop than a catering office because Rowan apparently had quite the green thumb, himself. Everything was just right in his garden in front and the lawn was springy and green.

Myrtle rang the bell and Rowan answered the door with alacrity. "Miss Myrtle! As I live and breathe! What a pleasure to see you today. And you've even brought a friend with you." He reached out his hand.

"Miles Bradford," said Miles with a polite smile.

Rowan took Miles's hand in both of his. "Any friend of Miss Myrtle's is a friend of mine. Goodness! Miss Myrtle taught me English and it seems like just yesterday."

"Unfortunately, it *wasn't* just yesterday," said Myrtle dryly. "At this point, I've been retired for more years than I taught."

"We'll just pretend that isn't true. Come in, come in! Let's get you all situated inside. What a treat!"

Rowan hustled them into a brightly-painted room filled with antique wooden furniture and needlepoint pillows.

"Now, what will it be? The one or the other?" asked Rowan.

Miles gave Myrtle a baffled look.

"What are the choices?" asked Myrtle as if she completely understood what Rowan was talking about.

"Bloody Marys or mimosas. Oh, actually, let me choose for you. I make the *best* Bloody Marys. The best!"

Miles looked faintly scandalized. "But it isn't even lunch yet."

Rowan waved his hand dismissively. "This is breakfast in a glass. I use real tomato juice with tomato bits in there. And there's celery and a lemon wedge. It's absolutely scrumptious."

Miles gave Myrtle a panicked glance.

Myrtle clucked at Rowan. "You know I only drink sherry and it's way too early in the day for a sherry. But thank you."

Rowan was crestfallen. Then he sprang up. "At least let me bring you a bite to eat. I have something wonderful in the back that I've been experimenting with for a fancy brunch that's coming up for out-of-town guests for an upcoming wedding. You'll love these!"

He dashed to the back of the house and Miles murmured to Myrtle, "If I'd started with a Bloody Mary, I'd have been napping the rest of the day."

"Rowan simply lives a livelier life than we do, that's all," said Myrtle briskly.

Rowan swept back into the room a moment later with a platter full of little round foods. "So *here* we have Mediterranean frittata muffins with lots of yummy veggies in them. And *here* we have squash and parmesan mini quiches. They will both just melt in your mouth."

He lay down a few napkins with *Rowan Blaine Catering* embossed on them and beamed at Myrtle and Miles. "You don't know how happy it makes me to see you both today." He put his hands over his mouth. "Oh goodness. Is this an *especially* special occasion we're planning? Perhaps I should have offered to bring out the champagne."

Miles turned a ruddy color and Myrtle snorted. "If you're talking about a wedding, then no. Miles is my friend. We're also both in garden club and are following up for Tippy on the silent auction plan."

Rowan gave them both sympathetic looks. "What a terrible mess that all is. Poor Lillian. The club is going through with the auction, then?"

"At the family's insistence," said Myrtle.

Rowan nodded thoughtfully. "Good for them. Lillian would have been the first one to say 'business as usual.' But then, those of us in this business know all about life's little curve balls. We're making food and floral arrangements for weddings, baptisms, golden anniversaries, and funerals. Life just keeps right on trucking."

"You're exactly right—Lillian would have wanted the auction to carry on," said Myrtle.

Miles said, "I suppose you knew her very well, then? Working in similar businesses in a small town?"

"Goodness, yes. Yes, I knew Lillian Johnson better than I knew my own family. Warts and all." He gave a rueful laugh and shook his head. "I tell you, that lady was a mess sometimes."

"And she could be very difficult to get along with," said Myrtle.

Miles said, "I'm just a bit curious. I didn't know her very well, considering I'm new to the club."

Rowan said, "Oh, I can tell you all about her. The one word I'd use to sum Lillian up is *artiste*. Lillian was an artist in every way. And yes, she was a perfectionist. But she never asked more of anyone than she did of herself. She felt personally responsible that each event she worked would be a tremendous success in every way."

"She was very complex," offered Myrtle, trying to get Rowan to be a little less-complimentary.

"People have a hard time understanding artists in general," said Rowan, waving his hand again to indicate the impossibility of the task. "Lillian was a consummate professional, as am I. From that perspective, we had gobs in common. We both cared passionately about our jobs and wanted everything to go perfectly."

"So the two of you got along well then," said Myrtle.

"Well, you know how perfectionists can be. Sometimes Lillian and I might have bumped heads a little, but we always had the greatest respect for each other."

Miles said, "It must have been quite a shock when you found out she was gone."

Rowan looked solemn. "It certainly was. I understand she was murdered the evening before and discovered in the morning. It's hard to believe that while I was busily working late and then going upstairs to my little dog that poor Lillian was fighting for her life. It makes me feel as if there must have been something I could have done to prevent this from happening."

"It's hard to imagine no one saw or heard anything," said Myrtle.

Rowan nodded enthusiastically. "Exactly! I was just telling someone the same thing. In a town like *Bradley* where everyone is mixed up in everyone else's business, it's hard to believe Lillian could meet such a terrible end. Of all nights for me to stay inside and work. It's just this major wedding I'm working on. Every time I come up with a fabulous menu, the bride calls me up and makes changes. I'm a nervous wreck! So I stayed up burning the midnight oil and coming up with another menu for the millionth time and didn't walk little Benji."

He gestured across the room to a tiny dog curled up in a chair. Myrtle had originally mistaken the creature for a particularly fluffy pillow.

"Of course, I hadn't actually seen Lillian for weeks. We've been working completely different events. I've been recruited for some out-of-town jobs," he said.

Miles raised his eyebrows. "I'm guessing that must be quite a coup."

Rowan tried and failed to look modest. "I've many very kind friends who do their best to spread the word about my catering."

"And Lillian wasn't working those jobs? I can only imagine she must have been professionally envious about losing those opportunities," said Myrtle.

Rowan clasped his hands together. "She wasn't pleased, but Lillian frequently *wasn't* pleased, was she? As I mentioned, she was such a perfectionist. That poor assistant of hers." He rolled his eyes dramatically.

"Bianca?" prompted Myrtle.

"The hapless Bianca, yes. I'm sure Lillian would have blamed any lost opportunities on Bianca. She frequently complained about her lack of productivity because of Bianca's ineptitude and pokiness." A smile played around Rowan's mouth at the memory.

"She was too slow?" asked Myrtle.

"I don't think it was as much that she was slow as the fact that Lillian, nine times out of ten, would completely *undo* everything Bianca had done. Lillian was never completely pleased with the arrangements Bianca came up with and was always pulling them apart. No wonder it took Bianca forever to finish. And Lillian could be sooo mean to Bianca. So completely harsh. A couple of times it crossed my mind to bring Bianca on board with me as an assistant. The poor lamb." Rowan clicked his tongue.

Miles cleared his throat. "But you didn't."

Rowan looked at him with wide eyes. "Of course not! It would have been professional suicide. Lillian would never have forgiven me for poaching one of her employees, no matter how much she complained about her. She'd have carped at me for ages and ages."

"She had a long memory, then," said Myrtle.

"Like an elephant! She held grudges like crazy. Honestly, I'm amazed Lillian didn't die of natural causes. She'd get so keyed up that I'd assumed she'd have had a heart attack long ago. She was so very uptight." He reached out a hand to Benji who'd woken up and trotted over to nuzzle Rowan.

Miles tentatively picked up a mini quiche and took a hesitant bite. He quickly took a larger bite next.

Rowan beamed at him.

Myrtle said, "Who do you think could have done such a thing to Lillian?"

Rowan said casually, "Oh her daughter, don't you think?"

"Annie? You think so?"

"Certainly. Well, I don't have any *evidence* to that effect or anything. It's just my gut reaction." He put a hand on his belly.

Myrtle mused, "I really didn't see Lillian with her daughter, I don't think."

Rowan's eyes were big again. "If you had, you wouldn't have forgotten it. They were like cats and dogs, those two. In fact, you wouldn't have even had to *see* them together . . . you could probably have *heard* them from half a mile away."

"What were their arguments over?" asked Miles curiously. "Annie doesn't seem so terrible to me."

"Of course she's not. She's a perfectly lovely young woman with a lot of promise who's going to be inspirational to a lot of America's young people as a wonderful teacher. But to Lillian, she was a dreadful disappointment," said Rowan.

"Just because she didn't want to be a florist?" asked Miles. "That seems very short-sighted of Lillian."

Rowan pursed his lips and considered this. "You're right. But the way I think it worked is that Lillian thought she was raising an apprentice. She had Annie over at that shop ringing up customers when she was just a wee thing. Had a stool so she could see over the counter. All the customers thought Annie was adorable, of course. She was sort of a draw. But I don't believe Annie even liked being in the shop back then. Her brother Martin was barely in the shop at all and Lillian seemed to fawn over him."

Myrtle said, "Obviously, Lillian had lower expectations for Martin."

Rowan shrugged. "It was one of those doting mother-son things. He was spoiled silly."

Miles said, "And then Annie decided she wanted to be a teacher instead of a florist."

"No, no, it all started before that. Lillian had Annie start doing arrangements for her. Just the really simple kind at first—you know, the bud vases for the sanctuaries in honor of a new baby . . . that sort of thing. But Lillian was *such* a perfectionist that she even found fault with the tiniest missteps of Annie's."

Myrtle frowned. "Ridiculous. Especially considering she was a child and Lillian was getting free labor."

Rowan nodded. "And Annie wasn't getting any positive feedback whatsoever, as far as I could tell. Only criticism. I'd drop by the shop and compliment Annie on one of her little arrangements. 'Oh, it's so beautiful, Annie! Such a wonderful job you did!' And her tiny face would just beam! She was *so* happy. But then Lillian would scowl at the poor little thing and tell her she hadn't put enough baby's breath in the bud vase. She was absolutely awful to her in every single way. Couldn't say a nice thing to save her own soul."

Miles said, "And Lillian wasn't the same with Martin?"

Rowan said, "Goodness, no. As far as Lillian was concerned, Martin was the bee's knees. He could do no wrong. Even though he *did* do wrong, of course. He was something of a heathen in high school, I think. Did you teach him, Miss Myrtle?"

"No, I didn't. Although I taught some of the older friends he ran around with. Little pagans, all of them," said Myrtle, making a face.

Rowan chuckled. "Too funny. Although I can't really say anything bad about Martin right now because he's paying me to handle the funeral reception for his mama."

"Really?" Myrtle raised her eyebrows. "He's turning down the church ladies with their casseroles? Lillian was an active member of the church and I'm sure the bereavement committee already had a complete plan for running Lillian's funeral reception."

"Oh, you *know* they did. With chicken divan and ham biscuits and all!" Rowan managed not to sound condescending when speaking of the church ladies' offerings. "But apparently, Martin wanted a bit of an upgrade in terms of the buffet." Rowan again tried and failed to look modest.

Myrtle said, "Well, that's going to create some grumblings at the church."

"Not that Martin attends, anyway," said Rowan. "So he'll be largely unaffected." He suddenly changed tack. His voice was slightly wheedling now. "Miss Myrtle, are you still writing your lovely stories for the newspaper?"

Myrtle straightened in her seat. "I most certainly am. Did you see my piece on Lillian?"

Rowan's eyes widened. "That was your article? Such an amazing story."

"I wrote the coverage on her murder *and* the write-up on her life," said Myrtle, looking smug.

Rowan said, "Now I hope I'm not stepping out of line, Miss Myrtle. But I would *love* for you to write a feature on my modest catering business for the paper. Doesn't the *Bugle* do write-ups or profiles of local businesses? They should!"

"I thought you had all the business you could handle," said Myrtle. "You're even catering events for other towns, for heaven's sake."

Rowan said, "Oh, but I'm a workaholic. Besides, who doesn't love seeing a write-up of themselves in the local newspaper? I'd be a celebrity, practically." He paused and said, "And I'd be sure to advertise. You know, as sort of a quid pro quo."

"I could tell Sloan. He's always looking for things to publish and definitely could use more advertising. Of course, *I* don't write those types of stories. It would have to be a junior reporter on the staff." Myrtle sniffed.

Miles gave her a look.

Rowan said quickly, "Naturally, you don't! But maybe you'd take a look at the story with your little red pen before it's published? Sometimes there are those tacky typos in articles, but never in yours."

Myrtle preened. "I suppose I could do that."

Rowan beamed at her. "Excellent!" Then he picked up a folder and gave Myrtle and Miles an apologetic look. "I'm so enjoying our chat, but I guess we should go over the catering details for the auction? I'd hate to have Tippy mad at me."

Myrtle said, "Of course we can." She pulled a small notebook out of her cavernous purse.

The next fifteen minutes, Rowan delved enthusiastically into the menu plan for the event, the chafing dishes he'd bring, and how he was planning on arranging the food in the space while Myrtle asked questions and jotted down notes. Miles nodded off, jerking back awake in alarm numerous times until it was time for them to leave right as Rowan's next clients rang the bell.

Chapter Twelve

Myrtle held out her hand for the keys as she and Miles walked toward the car. "I'm certainly not getting into a motor vehicle with someone who's falling asleep like Dozey from Snow White and the Seven Dwarfs."

Miles frowned. "There wasn't a Dozey."

"Of course there was! He constantly fell asleep, just as you did."

Miles said, "His name was Sleepy. I think you made an odd amalgam between Dopey and Sleepy."

"Whatever. All I know is that you don't need to be behind the wheel of a car." Myrtle held her hand out in a peremptory fashion and Miles reluctantly dropped the keys in it.

Myrtle slid behind the wheel and started up the car. She carefully backed out onto the road from Rowan's driveway. It was, in fact, such a very careful backup that by the time she'd executed it, a car had suddenly appeared on the road and honked at her.

Myrtle glared at it. "Speeders! Where on earth is Red Clover when one needs him?"

Miles yawned. "Trying to catch a murderer, I suppose." He rested his head on the passenger window as Myrtle sedately drove toward Magnolia Lane.

Myrtle gave him a dissatisfied look. "I thought we might talk about Rowan, but I can see that's not going to work."

"All I want to do is go back to bed," said Miles. "Maybe we can talk about Rowan later."

Myrtle said, "You should set an alarm for yourself or else you'll sleep the entire day and then you'll be up the entire night."

"At this point, even that sounds good. In fact, I might even sleep for 24 hours straight." He stifled another yawn.

"As long as you're ready for Lillian's funeral tomorrow morning. I'll need to write a story about it and maybe we'll have the chance to speak with her family again."

Miles snorted. "And have Martin pitch insurance."

"You should simply learn to say no. It's very easy to do." Myrtle pulled into Miles's driveway. "All right. I'll just walk home from here. Do get some sleep, Miles. Your insomnia is cramping my sleuthing."

Miles nodded as he stumbled toward his front door.

"The keys!" Myrtle dangled them and Miles turned around to collect them, dropping them twice before finally making it to the house.

Back home, Myrtle was closing her front door when Pasha slipped in behind her, blinking up at her fetchingly.

"Hungry, Pasha?" crooned Myrtle. "What a smart kitty you are. Let's have something to eat."

She opened a can of tuna for the black cat and made herself a bowl of soup. After Pasha finished her food, she hopped up in the chair next to Myrtle's and purred at her as Myrtle finished off her soup.

Usually Pasha wanted to leave just as quickly as she arrived, but this time she appeared to want to hang out. Myrtle sat in her recliner with her book and the cat curled up on her sofa as the two relaxed for hours.

The next morning, Myrtle woke early, eyes flying open. She'd forgotten to evaluate the condition of her funeral outfit before turning in. She slid out of bed and hurried to her closet, flipping through elastic-waisted pants and button-front blouses before finding it. Amazingly, the outfit looked to be in good condition. Usually, ghastly things happened to her funeral clothing in her closet. It was as if gremlins stole in there and mucked the garments through the outdoor garbage bin.

Because of her early-morning panic over her attire, she was up for good. There was no trying to go back to sleep after waking up like that. The problem was that it was exceedingly early in the day. The paper wasn't in her driveway yet, which was most annoying. Pasha was still out hunting in the darkness and didn't come when Myrtle opened her kitchen window in invitation. There was nothing left to do but cook, even though Myrtle knew she was going to be eating a lot of heavy foods not much later in the day at Lillian's funeral reception.

She'd just cooked up a plate of scrambled eggs, a pot of grits, and a bunch of bacon when her doorbell rang. Myrtle smiled and walked to the door to see Miles.

"Did you end up turning in at five o'clock last evening?" she asked.

He shook his head. "I was able to stay up until eight. But I woke up early, anyway."

Myrtle peered at him. "You do seem more awake than you were yesterday, at least. Well, come on in."

Miles followed her to the kitchen and surveyed the large amount of food. "Did you know I was coming?"

Myrtle shrugged. "There wasn't anything else for me to do, so I decided to cook." She made Miles a plate of eggs, bacon, and grits.

Miles ate a forkful. "This is all good, Myrtle. See, you really just need to stick to simple foods. You've *mastered* simple foods."

"But that's not *fun* to cook. I like the creative part of cooking."

Miles didn't answer, continuing to eat his breakfast.

Myrtle snapped her fingers. "We do have something we can do. I have a *Tomorrow's Promise* taped that we can see after breakfast."

"Good. That should take up a whole forty-five minutes." Miles looked morosely at the clock and the earliness of the hour.

"Well, the newspaper should have come by then, and we'll be able to work on the crossword puzzle together. Maybe we can even do the sudoku."

Miles said, "The sudoku? You never work those."

"If I'm killing time I might. And then it might be time to get ready for the funeral."

Miles looked doubtful. "Perhaps. If we spend hours working the puzzles."

Somehow, they managed to fill the hours before Lillian's funeral. They left early for the service and were the only ones there besides the family.

This made Miles nervous. "We shouldn't have come so early. I feel as if we're intruding on the family."

"We're simply making sure we're here promptly to pay our respects. Oh look, Martin's coming over."

Miles sighed. "He'll use this event as an excellent excuse to sell life insurance. Or funeral insurance or something."

"Nonsense," said Myrtle and then smiled a somber it's-a-funeral smile at Martin as he approached them. "Martin, everything looks lovely here. Lillian would have been so pleased."

He beamed at them. "Do you think so? Mama was always hard to please, so those words are high praise." He swooped in to give Myrtle a hug and bobbed his head at Miles. "I just wanted to say that y'all are more than welcome to sit under the tent."

Miles looked alarmed. "Oh no. No, we wouldn't want to sit in the family seating."

Martin waved his hand. "There really isn't much family and it's ridiculous for the two of you to stand in the hot sun for ages. Please."

Miles opened his mouth as if to argue the point and Myrtle cut in smoothly, "That is just lovely of you, Martin, thank you. We'll do that."

He nodded and then looked across the cemetery. "Here's Rowan. I should check in with him about the food for later. You'll both be at the reception, I hope?"

"Of course we will," said Myrtle.

Martin smiled at them and then hurried off to speak with Rowan as Myrtle pulled Miles's jacket sleeve.

"Come on. For heaven's sake, you act as if you *want* to stand in the broiling sun for over an hour," said Myrtle. "Age has at least a few privileges." A minute later, they sat in folding chairs in the last row of the tent.

"Look at all of the floral arrangements," said Miles quietly. "Bianca must have really had to knock herself out to come up with all of these."

Myrtle said in a tart voice, "She probably works faster now that Lillian isn't breathing down her neck telling her all the things she's doing wrong. And these look very nice. She made them very Southern-looking with the camellia blooms and magnolia leaves."

Fifteen minutes later, there were tons of people surrounding Lillian's grave. Miles raised his eyebrows. "After all the descriptions of Lillian, I somehow had the impression she wasn't exactly going to be missed. But the entire town seems to have turned out for her funeral."

"There you're wrong," said Myrtle in her stage whisper that could likely be heard a couple of rows ahead of them. "They're here for the reception afterward. Rowan Blaine makes absolutely fabulous food. Besides, there will be tons of opportunity for them to gossip, which is what the town of Bradley likes best." She bumped her leg into Miles's. "Look over there."

Miles pushed his glasses farther up his nose and peered through them. "At Erma?"

"Certainly *not* at Erma. We must always try to avoid looking at Erma. She sometimes sees it as a cue to engage in conversation. No, I mean the church ladies near her. See how sullen they look? They're staring daggers at Martin. You absolutely don't cut out the church ladies when they're planning on running a funeral reception for you."

"Thanks for the tip," said Miles dryly.

Myrtle said, "I wonder if their resentment will carry over to avoiding Rowan's food? I doubt it." She continued looking around. "There's Tallulah. Wow, she looks pretty rough today."

"It's a funeral, after all. There should be plenty of people looking rough."

"Except Tallulah and Lillian weren't exactly best friends. And Tallulah looks like someone who didn't sleep last night," said Myrtle.

Miles pushed his glasses up his nose. "I'll be the judge of that, since I'm an expert." He looked reflectively at Tallulah who'd made the unfortunate decision to wear black and not wear makeup. "Actually, she does look a little sleep-deprived."

"And she keeps looking over at Red." Myrtle pursed her lips thoughtfully.

Miles frowned. "In what way?" He peered over at Tallulah.

"I don't mean in a *romantic* way. She looks like she has something on her mind. Look how antsy she is."

Tallulah was a ball of restless energy. She was moving from one foot to the other and shifting her arms around. Her gaze would rest on Red and then flit off to someone else. She also craned her neck to look around her as if to see who else was there. Then her gaze returned to Red

"Maybe she feels guilty. Could she really have been that upset over Yard of the Month?" asked Miles.

Myrtle said, "Or else she knows something. After all, she was right next door to Lillian. It seems to me that she might have seen something. She strikes me as a neighbor very much like Erma. One who doesn't have a lot to do and spends days glued to the window."

Miles turned to look at Erma and Myrtle snapped, "For heaven's sake! Don't look at her. It will only encourage her."

A soloist started singing the Lord's Prayer and Myrtle and Miles stopped talking and sat solemnly through the rather long service. Martin looked relaxed but solemn. His sister sat stiffly as if forced to be there. Bianca, Lillian's employee, was also in attendance and kept looking fretfully at the floral arrangements as if spotting some flaw that no one else could see.

There was a string quartet, another solo, eulogies, and a full sermon. It was fortunate Miles had somewhat caught up on his sleep and didn't doze off. Myrtle kept watching Tallulah watch Red.

Finally, the service wound to a close.

"Thank goodness," breathed Miles. "Now what's the plan?"

"Well, we're definitely heading to the reception. But I'd like to see if Tallulah ends up speaking to Red. Maybe we can hover close enough to Red so we can overhear if she approaches him, but not *too* close so Red ends up speaking with us and scares Tallulah off."

Miles considered this. "What approximate proximity are we talking about?"

"Just follow me," said Myrtle.

"Shouldn't we speak with the family first?" asked Miles, looking uncomfortable. He was always one for following correct protocol.

"We'll see them at the reception," said Myrtle. "Come on."

They got within a few feet of Red and he raised his eyebrows and gave them a nod. There was an older woman who had just engaged him in conversation. Tallulah, who had been heading in Red's direction, hesitated as she spotted the woman with him. She instead started fiddling with her phone while keeping an eye on Red.

The older woman sounded cranky. "I just think it's dreadful, Red. Something *must* be done about my neighbors."

Myrtle rolled her eyes at Miles.

Red said in his most patient voice, "Remind me again what the issue is, Miz Patty?"

Patty said petulantly, "I thought you'd remember. I've spoken with you about it before."

Myrtle reflected that Red's patience was likely becoming strained as she saw a patch of red crawl out of his collar and up his neck. "I'm sure I'll remember as soon as you tell me, Miz Patty. It's just been crazy-busy at the department lately."

Patty said, "It's about those children who live next door to me. Or, rather, their completely inattentive parents. They haven't been to school at *all*, lately. It used to be just one or two days a week and now it's all the time!"

As Patty continued ranting about the neighbors, Myrtle watched Tallulah. She stopped fiddling with her phone and looked again at Red before sitting on a bench. She appeared to want to wait out Red's conversation.

But Patty didn't seem in any hurry to walk away. Plus, the more she talked about the neighbors, the more grievances she came up with. Myrtle rolled her eyes at Miles.

Red finally tried to stem the tide. "Miz Patty, again, I appreciate your letting me know. I agree the parents could use a talking to, whether from me or the school. I'll check in with the school first to see what I can find out. Are you sure the kids aren't being homeschooled?"

Patty blinked. This possibility had apparently not occurred to her.

Red said gently, "It may be that's all that's going on. But I'll be sure to follow-up on it, to make sure. It's been good speaking with you, but I'm afraid I've got to head out . . . I have a meeting I need to attend."

Myrtle made a face at Miles. This was not part of the plan.

As Red hurried by he said, "Hi, Miles. Mama." In a dash, he was at his police car.

"Pooh," said Myrtle. She looked over at Tallulah and she looked as frustrated as Myrtle did. "Let's go see if Tallulah will tell us what's up."

Miles groaned. "Must we?"

"There's something up, isn't there? We should find out what it is." Myrtle started setting off, but stopped as someone tapped her on the shoulder behind her.

She spun to see Erma standing there, sniffing a bit.

Myrtle jumped and Miles took a step backward to impose better personal space boundaries.

Erma said, "Wasn't it such a lovely service? Such a *pity* Lillian couldn't see what a nice funeral she had. And I'm so glad I was able to make it—I had this terrible stomachache this morning. Seriously, I don't know *what* was wrong, but I was totally wracked with pain."

Now Miles took *another* step backward and patted his suit pocket for his hand sanitizer.

"Yes, it was a lovely service," said Myrtle hastily. "Unfortunately, Miles and I need to leave, though. Now." She glanced over at Tallulah, but she was already gone.

After successfully escaping from Erma, they climbed into Miles's car and he set off. Myrtle added thoughtfully, "I feel like I want to know more about Martin. There's just something that seems a little off about him."

"The way he tries to hawk insurance at every available opportunity?" asked Miles.

"You're far too obsessed with that, Miles. And no, it has more to do with his background and his money. With his relationship with his mother. I really feel as though he must be hiding something. It's a pity I didn't teach him."

Miles said, "I'd think you'd be relieved you didn't teach him. He sounds like he might have been something of a pistol."

"Oh, I'd have been able to manage him, have no fear of that." Myrtle snapped her fingers. "I know. I could speak with my friend, Carolyn. I've known her since back when she was a middle school librarian. She lived right next door to Lillian then."

"Before Tallulah lived there? Or on the other side?" asked Miles.

"On the other side. She might be able to give me some more of Martin's backstory and maybe more about Lillian and Annie, too," said Myrtle. "We'll run by the public library after the reception. She's helping out there now. Information was always her forte."

As expected, the funeral reception was rather lavish. "Rowan has outdone himself," muttered Myrtle.

"It looks more like a wedding reception than a funeral reception," said Miles, glancing around.

Rowan had apparently gone all-out. There were photographs of Lillian interspersed with sterling silver chafing dishes and serving spoons. The foods were upscale spins on typical Southern funeral foods. Martin must not have spared any cost. Myrtle and Miles filled their plates.

Miles murmured, "I had no idea the flower business was so profitable."

"Or is this an example of overspending by someone who regularly does it?" asked Myrtle.

The bottom floor of Martin's tremendous house was completely full of Bradley residents. Myrtle scowled at them. "It's very hard to find the family when there are so many vultures in here."

"Vultures? Really? I thought the appropriate term was 'mourners.'"

Myrtle said, "Not when they're so clearly here for the food." She frowned. "Some of these people seem a little intoxicated."

Miles shrugged. "Maybe they're simply high on life since they've just left a funeral. What's the German term? *Schadenfreude*?"

"I think they're high on more than life. Look at them."

Sure enough, there seemed to be a portion of the gathering that was quite raucous. They were getting louder and louder, too, with both their conversation and their laughter.

Miles looked over at them. "On the upside, I think we've located Martin."

"He's serving alcohol here?" Myrtle raised her eyebrows. "For a Bradley funeral, that's really unheard of."

"And expensive," added Miles.

"Well, we're not going to imbibe. We need to have all our faculties for investigating."

Miles cast a regretful look at the counter that was serving as a bar.

"Let's find Annie. I'm not positive Martin would even register our condolences if we were to give them to him," said Myrtle.

Chapter Thirteen

B ut Annie proved difficult to find. Myrtle and Miles made a couple of unsuccessful passes downstairs in case Annie was on the move. But she was nowhere to be found.

Myrtle said, "Let's split up. I'll check outside and you can check upstairs."

Miles balked. "I'm not going upstairs. That seems rather off-limits. The family quarters."

"It's not a family. It's only Martin. But all right. *I'll* go up-stairs and you go outside. We can text each other if we find her." Someone jostled Myrtle, spilling wine on her. "Watch it!" she snapped at the middle-aged man. He reddened, mumbled an apology, and hastily retreated. "Something always happens to my funeral outfit," she growled.

Myrtle headed for an elaborate staircase under a tremen-dous crystal chandelier while Miles set off through a couple of French doors to what looked to be an amazing deck with lake views.

The elaborate staircase was steeper than Myrtle anticipated and required a certain amount of athleticism to ascend. She boosted herself with her cane and it thumped on the marble as she went. She knew if anyone questioned her about being up-stairs, she could easily get away with acting confused. It was an excellent trick and she'd occasionally rely on it. No one would challenge an octogenarian on that point, after all.

But no one seemed to be paying attention at all as the party downstairs became louder and louder.

Myrtle paused at the top of the stairs, slightly winded, and peered down the long hallway with what appeared to be a dozen or more doors. The place was more like a hotel than a house. All the doors seemed to be open, at least. She slowly walked down the hall.

Myrtle had passed several empty bedrooms when she came upon what appeared to be a library. She raised her eyebrows. She wouldn't necessarily have pegged Martin as a reader. She'd have to ask Carolyn, her school librarian friend, about that. Myrtle, never able to resist a library, walked in.

"Hi, Miss Myrtle," said a quiet voice.

Myrtle startled and turned around to see Annie on a leather sofa behind her.

"Oh, goodness," said Myrtle. "Annie, I'm sorry to disturb you, today of all days." She decided she didn't need her old lady act with Annie. Annie might not believe it. Instead, she said, "I heard about Martin's library and I thought I'd take a look. I can't seem to pass up a library."

Annie smiled weakly at her. "That's okay, Miss Myrtle. It's probably better for me to talk to somebody, anyway. I just came up here to be quiet for a few minutes and then things got so loud downstairs that I didn't want to go back down. What's going on down there?"

"Alcohol," said Myrtle simply.

Annie made a face. "I told Martin not to offer an open bar but he never listens to me. Well, I'm definitely not going back downstairs now." She hesitated. "Like I said, I probably needed to talk to somebody, though. I'm glad it's you."

To Myrtle's alarm, Annie burst into tears. Myrtle stood up and looked frantically around for a box of tissues. There were none to be seen, so she pawed through her tremendous purse until she found a packet of travel tissues buried somewhere near the bottom. She thrust them at Annie and made comforting sounds until Annie finally stopped crying.

"Sorry," said Annie behind several tissues. "I think it's all just hit me now. Mama's death, I mean. And I feel terrible about it—the way she died, the fact we weren't on better terms, all of it. I also feel really guilty that it didn't make me upset to hear Mama was dead. I felt . . . relieved." She stared down miserably at the wad of tissues in her hand.

Myrtle made some tut-tutting noises. "Well, of course you felt that way. Death affects everyone in different ways on different days. But I'd think your mother also would have felt badly too, if you'd been able to ask her. She'd have been sorry she hadn't developed a better relationship with you. That was more of her responsibility and less of yours."

Annie gave her a grateful look. "Do you think so? Thanks, Miss Myrtle."

They sat quietly for a few moments. Myrtle glanced around the library and thought all the books seemed to be in excellent condition. Most of them appeared to be unread, especially the books of a more-serious and literary nature. However, there were many shelves of paperbacks that looked quite dog-eared. Perhaps Martin *was* a reader, after all.

Myrtle said, "I did have a question for you. It's about a neighbor of yours."

Annie smiled. "Our former neighbor? Carolyn? Oh, she's wonderful. She's one of the reasons I enjoyed school and reading as much as I did. She always had such terrific recommendations for things to read. She has little grandchildren now and I bet she's developing a love of reading in them, too."

Myrtle said, "Carolyn is a terrific librarian and book-lover. But I actually meant your neighbor on the *other* side."

Annie made a face. "You mean Tallulah. She's dreadful."

"I ran into her at the store," said Myrtle.

"I'm sorry to hear that," said Annie with a grimace.

Myrtle chuckled. "She did seem a little peculiar. I got the impression she and your mother didn't get along very well."

"You might say that. *I* might say they fought like cats and dogs," said Annie.

"Tallulah didn't mention that, though. She said they didn't see eye to eye on a Yard of the Month award for their neighborhood," said Myrtle.

Annie snorted. "Sure. Maybe that was one of the *minor* things they argued about. But I can assure you it was a lot more complicated than that. Mama had offers from a developer for the lot that was behind her house and Tallulah's."

"That sounds like quite a spacious lot."

"It is. The developer was actually going to divide it in half and put up two homes," said Annie.

"I have the feeling Tallulah didn't much care for the idea."

"She was livid," said Annie with a faint smile. "It's kind of funny now, but it was making Mama furious the way Tallulah was behaving. Mama said it was her land to do whatever she wanted to do with and that Tallulah was just lucky Mama hadn't gotten a decent offer from a developer up until that point."

"Tallulah wanted the land to stay undeveloped," said Myrtle thoughtfully.

Annie said, "Absolutely. Mama said she wanted her privacy and Tallulah thought if the developer put these two-story houses right in her backyard that they'd be able to see right into her property."

"Tallulah could simply have installed some privacy landscaping. I have some of that at my house. Tall bushes and trees and whatnot. I have a problematic neighbor, as well." Myrtle made a face at the thought of Erma.

"Apparently, Tallulah wasn't interested in redesigning her yard. She wanted it the way it was because she grew vegetables in the summer and didn't want all the shade that would come with planting large bushes and trees."

"She was in quite a pickle, then," said Myrtle.

Annie looked startled. "You don't think Tallulah would have killed Mama over something like that?"

"I don't know. But she sure didn't want me to know the real reason she was feuding with your mother. Yard of the Month, indeed!" Myrtle sniffed. "And what will happen with the real estate deal now?"

Annie frowned. "I haven't really thought about it. I don't think Mama had actually signed the papers yet. She was speaking with the developers in the vacant lot, which is how Tallulah found out about it. I guess we're under no obligation to go through with it. But I have the feeling Martin will be all over it. In fact, he's so unsentimental, I bet he'd sell Mama's house, to boot. Then the developer could put up two *more* houses. She had a big lot, too."

Myrtle said, "That means, if Tallulah *did* murder Lillian, she didn't gain a thing. I don't believe it's something Tallulah could have counted on."

Annie shook her head. "No, of course not. It was silly of me to even think it." She paused. "Unless it wasn't planned. What if Tallulah went over to Mama's house to speak with her again about the development? Maybe Mama made her angry and she killed her in the heat of the moment. She could easily have slipped over there and back without anyone seeing her."

"You're saying it might have been manslaughter."

Annie said, "That's right." She sighed. "Although I have a tough time believing Tallulah could have done that. I mean, I never really liked the woman, but I sure wouldn't have said she was capable of doing something like that. Don't pay any attention to me. I'm just overtired and stressed out."

Myrtle stood and said, "I do hope you can get some rest soon. Lack of sleep definitely never helps. My friend Miles has been exhausted for days and he's been *most* out of whack."

"Thanks, Miss Myrtle," said Annie with a smile.

Myrtle found her way back downstairs where the funeral reception was even more cacophonous. The drinking was certainly loosening everyone up. She scowled at a few of the loudest offenders and they had the decency to look abashed. One was a former student of hers and he practically sank beneath a table when she leveled her glare at him.

But Miles was nowhere to be seen. Myrtle knew he hadn't found Annie, so what on earth could be keeping him?

She walked outside on the deck where there were several revelers and an entire bottle of wine. Miles was curled up in a deck chair, dead asleep despite the volume of the people next to him.

Myrtle strode up and impatiently grabbed Miles by the shoulder. "Miles!" she hissed.

He sleepily opened his eyes and then glanced around, looking alarmed. He sat abruptly up, blinking furiously to clear the sleep away.

"I must still be exhausted," he muttered.

"Considering you fell deeply asleep at what's turning out to be a bacchanalian event, I'd agree with you," said Myrtle tartly. "Let's get out of here. Things are out of control."

"Do you think I could get a Coke here?" asked Miles.

"I'm sure they must have them as mixers for alcoholic beverages. Although I'm not sure I want you to drive again," said Myrtle.

"Oh, I'm awake now," said Miles dryly. "Waking up in that manner made me fully alert in seconds. But I'd like to ward off another nap attack and I believe you mentioned we'd be heading over to the public library. A Coke might be in order." He glanced across the crowded, lively living room. "I'll brave the bar to find one."

"I'll meet you by the car," said Myrtle briskly.

Back in the car, Miles said, "Did you find Annie?"

"I did. She was upstairs in Martin's library."

Miles's eyes grew wide. "A library? Martin?"

"I was surprised, too, but then I remembered the fact that my friend Carolyn had been a good influence as both his neighbor and his middle school librarian. I'll admit many of his books looked as if they were there for show, but there were quite a few well-thumbed paperbacks, as well."

Miles asked, "What did you find out from Annie? Anything on her brother? I find it very difficult to believe he could purchase a lake house like that by hawking insurance in a small town."

"No, we really didn't talk about Martin much, although I sense he's not Annie's most-favorite person. We spoke more about Tallulah," said Myrtle.

Miles headed to downtown Bradley. "Is that stemming from the 'Conversation that Wasn't' at the funeral today?"

"Exactly. She clearly wanted to speak with Red. Red was even more clearly tied up with the annoying woman worried about truancy. And Tallulah was very nervous. She's hiding something and I figure it might be a guilty conscience."

"Over Yard of the Month?" Miles rolled his eyes.

"No, over something far more important to Tallulah. Annie told me her mother owned that large, wooded lot behind both her house and Tallulah's. Apparently, she'd been talking to developers for years, but never received a good offer. Until lately."

Miles raised his eyebrows. "I'm guessing Tallulah wasn't happy about having a house behind hers."

"Apparently, the developer was going to divide it into two lots. There was to be a two-story house directly behind Tallulah's and she was worried about privacy and so forth."

Miles said, "And Tallulah decided to remove her problem by removing Lillian?"

"It sounds a bit unplanned to me. After all, Tallulah couldn't count on the fact Martin and Annie wouldn't simply sell the property after their mother was gone. But Tallulah could have gone over to speak with Lillian, had an argument, and killed her out of anger," said Myrtle.

"And now she wants to confess to Red. The guilt is killing her?" asked Miles.

Myrtle shrugged. "Maybe she's had to work up the courage to confess."

Miles pulled up in front of the library. "I should have brought my library book with me." He looked gloomily at the building. "It will be overdue tomorrow."

"Renew it." Myrtle carefully swung out of Miles's car and started thumping with her cane as she walked up the library steps.

Miles hurried to keep up. "I've already renewed it. Twice."

"Well then, it mustn't be very good if it's taking you that long to read the thing. Pick something else out while we're in here."

Miles said slowly, "But then they'll see I have a book that's about to be overdue. It looks greedy for me to take out another book when I have a book at home I haven't finished."

"Don't be so fretful, Miles! Clearly, it's a subpar, very inadequate book. We've had this conversation before. You worry too much about what others think of you. Besides, Carolyn isn't the sort to pass judgement on a book on the brink of being overdue. Ask her for a recommendation. And do come on."

The library was one of Myrtle's favorite places in town. It had a delightful reading nook in front of a fireplace. The selection of books was well-curated. And it was a good place to speak with librarians who knew things.

Carolyn Segers was just wrapping up with a patron and greeted Myrtle and Miles. "Perfect timing! It's finally quiet here. How have you been?" She sparkled with a twinkly smile and a pink blouse with beaded flowers, cheerful sequined dangling earrings, and a cute pair of multicolored flats.

Myrtle beamed at her. "Oh, just fine. And I'm glad it's quiet here because Miles and I have a question for you."

Miles turned red and started stammering.

Myrtle gave him a reproving look. "I really meant we had a question about Martin, Miles. But since you've clearly leapt to conclusions, why don't you ask Carolyn for a book recommendation?" She turned to Carolyn and said, "Miles is rather anxious because he's about to have an overdue book. The book hasn't been engaging, though, and he wondered if you had a good recommendation."

Miles quickly added, "And I'm bringing the overdue book tomorrow to return it. And pay the fine."

"Which will be all of a few cents." Myrtle rolled her eyes.

Carolyn said, "Don't worry, you're not the only one with overdue books! What kinds of books do you like reading?"

Myrtle said, "I think the problem is that he's attracted to really boring books and then he runs into trouble finishing them.

Maybe he needs the kind of book he usually *doesn't* read and *doesn't* like."

Miles looked at Myrtle coldly. "Or maybe a really riveting book that is something I *would* read."

"What do you usually enjoy?" asked Carolyn.

"World War II nonfiction," said Miles. "But nothing too dry."

"Would you be open to reading some good World War II fiction?" she asked, tilting her head thoughtfully.

Miles looked a bit startled, as if he somehow hadn't realized there might be such a thing. "I'd could try."

"And if it's a bit gritty from time to time is that all right?" asked Carolyn.

Miles nodded. "It's war, after all."

They followed Carolyn into the stacks and she pulled out *The Boat Runner* by Devin Murphy. "See what you think," she said.

Miles looked a lot more relaxed now. "Thanks," he said with a smile.

Myrtle said, "I actually had a question for you, Carolyn. I'm sure you've heard about poor Lillian's death. Actually, you might even have been at the funeral reception for a little while, but it was so crowded it would have been easy to miss you."

Carolyn shook her head. "I sure did hear about Lillian. Such an awful thing. I couldn't make the funeral or reception because I was working."

"I know you used to be next-door neighbors up until fairly recently. I was wondering if she might have been a difficult person to be neighbors with," said Myrtle.

Carolyn said, "Oh, she wasn't too bad. She did such a wonderful job with her yard and it always looked lovely. And I was very fond of her children. Martin was a great reader."

Myrtle said, "Why do I have the feeling that he was a great reader because of you? Lillian didn't strike me as much of a reader."

"Maybe I helped a little. He'd always come knocking on my door when he was a little guy and would go through all the children's books I'd have out. Then he'd solemnly borrow one and take it for a couple of days and trade it out for something else."

Miles frowned. "This is Martin *Johnson*, right?"

Carolyn said, "It might sound a little surprising, but it's true. And Lillian always had a soft spot for Martin."

"Not so much for Annie, though?" asked Myrtle.

Carolyn looked a little sad. "Unfortunately, I think they had something of a more complicated relationship. Lillian could be very stern and not only with her daughter. I also overheard Lillian being rather rough on her employee when she'd come over."

"Sounds likely," said Miles.

"Was Martin any different as he grew older?" asked Miles. "He somehow doesn't seem the bookish, sensitive sort anymore."

Carolyn said, "He has a pretty grandiose lifestyle now, hasn't he? No, I didn't see any signs when he was younger that he'd turn out quite as he has. He did run with a rough crowd in middle school, though. I never heard of his getting into any trouble, though, even though the other boys did. I think Lillian kept on top of both of the kids."

Myrtle asked, "And how about Tallulah? What do you know about her?"

Carolyn considered this before diplomatically answering, "She's apparently quite an excellent golfer. At least, that's what I hear. And she did keep a nice yard."

Myrtle said, "We've heard she and Lillian had a disagreement recently."

Carolyn frowned and said, "I don't really know about any argument, but I can only guess it had to do with the land sale Lillian was planning. She told me about it one day when I saw her in town. She said she'd had quite a good offer from a developer and had been trying to sell that parcel of land for ages. When she was telling me about it, though, I couldn't help but think Tallulah couldn't have been too happy about it. After all, some of that land was directly behind her house."

There were suddenly a lot of chipper, small voices and Carolyn said, "Oh, we'd better get your book checked out. Storytime just let out and soon they'll all be with their mamas at the circulation desk."

Chapter Fourteen

A few minutes later, Myrtle and Miles were walking back down the library steps to his car.

Miles pulled carefully out of the parking spot. "I'm not sure we really learned anything new, did we?"

"We learned there are good World War II novels out there as long as you're willing to read something that might occasionally be gritty," said Myrtle.

"Aside from that, though? I guess we had more confirmation about Lillian and Tallulah's disagreement."

Myrtle said, "And don't forget, some more insight into Martin's background and character. I wanted to know more about what makes Martin, Martin."

"And you succeeded in that?" asked Miles in a dubious voice.

"I think so. I think he's a lot smarter than we realize. After all, he's been a reader most of his life. It might suit him to play the good old boy when he's trying to sell insurance, but I have to wonder if he's just pulling the wool over our eyes altogether," said Myrtle.

Miles gave Myrtle a sidelong glance. "I'm hoping you're feeling like a break. It's been a very long day already, considering we were up early. I was thinking about going home. I could read my new book."

Myrtle said, "That's fine, only because I need to write up my coverage of Lillian's funeral and reception for the paper. Perhaps I should check in with Wanda, too, and see if she has any other information for me."

Miles pulled into Myrtle's driveway and stopped the car. "How do you plan on doing that? You pretty much have to drive to check in with her. And she doesn't have a phone."

"She *does* have a phone. The phone Sloan gave her."

Miles said, "But she hardly even charges it because Crazy Dan doesn't pay the electric bill."

"Maybe I'll be lucky this time. After all, you slipped her some money. Maybe she paid her bill."

Miles looked pleased. "So that's it for today? We'll go our separate ways and meet up tomorrow morning? Hopefully not at 3 a.m.?"

Myrtle said, "No, let's go out for supper. I want to hash things out some more and I do better when talking it through with my loyal sidekick than with Pasha."

Myrtle's loyal sidekick made a face. "Can we at least make it something of an early night?"

"If you'd like to. Although I must say I think it's counterproductive to do so, considering how early you end up getting up." Myrtle opened her door and grabbed her cane. "Just call me later when you're ready to head out."

Myrtle wrote her story of the funeral quickly, carefully putting in all the details. She emailed the article to Sloan and called Wanda on the phone.

The phone rang several times, which Myrtle thought was a promising sign. Surely, the phone wouldn't ring if it wasn't charged. She smiled as she heard a gritty voice and then frowned again. It appeared to be Wanda's voice mail.

"Ain't here. Leave message," it gruffly instructed.

At the tone, Myrtle said, "Wanda, it's Myrtle. Please call when you get this message. I'd like to check in with you." She hung up and scowled at her phone. When it instantly started ringing, she jumped.

"Wanda?" she asked.

There was a pause and then a chuckle. "I didn't realize Wanda chatted on the phone."

Myrtle smiled as she heard her daughter-in-law's voice. Her smile grew when she heard Jack's in the background, making truck noises. "How is the smartest, best little boy in the world today?"

"Jack is having a big day," said Elaine with a laugh.

"That means *you're* having a big day, too."

"Exactly." Elaine paused. "I know you're busy over there, but could I ask you a favor?"

"Yes, I'll keep him," said Myrtle promptly. "I bought him a toy ambulance the other day and I've been dying to give it to him."

Elaine said, "Oh, sorry! I meant a different favor. Although you can definitely keep Jack if you'd like to for a few minutes while I run a couple of errands."

"Perfect! He and I can play trucks together," said Myrtle complacently.

"Great! That will let me run to the post office and the grocery store. Do you need anything from either place?" asked Elaine solicitously.

"Not a thing," said Myrtle.

"All right then." She paused again. "And this favor of mine. May I run it by?"

Myrtle raised her eyebrows. A favor to drop off? Her eyes narrowed suspiciously. "Naturally. What *is* the favor, though?"

"I don't think I've mentioned it to you, although I've spoken with Sloan about it." Elaine's voice grew bubbly and Myrtle winced. She knew what was coming, then.

"I think Sloan might have said something to me about it, now that I think about it. Something to do with literature?" asked Myrtle.

"Yes! I've been writing poetry and short stories. Oh Myrtle, it's been so much fun! And it's a cheap hobby that only requires a pencil and paper. I can do it while Jack is playing with his trucks. It's been the best thing ever."

Myrtle's heart sank. Elaine really seemed to have become quickly invested in this one.

"Of course you can run it by. You want me to edit it for you?" Myrtle crossed her fingers. It would be much easier to be merely looking for grammar and punctuation errors and not at whatever horribly flawed content Elaine brought to her.

"Well, that too, but mostly I want to know what you *think*. You're the one who knows English inside and out. You're the one who taught great works of literature through the years. You can quote all the top authors and poets. I want your opinion on what *I've* written."

Myrtle grimaced. She made her voice as pleasant as possible as she said, "I'd be honored to take a look, Elaine."

"Jack and I will be right over then! I'll just throw a few things in a bag for him." Elaine sounded breathless in her happiness and Myrtle wretchedly hung up the phone. It was easier when Elaine's horrid hobbies were things that could be thrown in a closet like knitting or photography or sculpting. Much harder when one had to critique something.

To distract herself from her pending doom, Myrtle pulled out chocolate chip cookies and made some lemonade from a mix. Then she opened her coat closet and got out the toy ambulance she'd gotten at the consignment shop. It was nearly as big as Jack and in perfect condition . . . aside from the fact that the siren appeared to no longer be working.

When the doorbell rang, Myrtle squared her shoulders and opened the front door. Jack's little face beamed up at her and she leaned over to give him a big hug. "Jack! How's the best boy ever?"

Elaine was right behind him, bearing a canvas bag full of snacks and toys. She also held a folder that likely carried her scribblings. She smiled at Myrtle. "Thanks *so* much for this. I know you have a lot going on right now with Lillian's death."

"It's no bother to me a bit," lied Myrtle. "I'll try to have feedback ready for you before long."

Elaine said, "And be sure not to sugar-coat it! Really. I want real feedback so I can improve. If it's awful, tell me it's awful."

But her eyes were shining in a way that indicated Elaine felt her writing was actually rather good and not awful in the slightest.

Myrtle nodded and forced a smile. She reached out her hand and Jack slid his small one into hers and smiled up at her. "Are you ready for a snack? And a surprise?"

His eyes grew wide and he nodded.

Elaine said, "Oh, he hasn't had a nap yet so feel free to turn on the TV after a while if he starts running down. I know you don't usually do that, but he might run out of steam soon. I'll try to hurry with my errands."

"Don't hurry," said Myrtle. "I'd like to visit with Jack for a while." She said, "By the way, you've done a good job lately online with all the photos you've done for the paper." It would be best to give her a compliment for *something*. And the photos hadn't had as many pictures of Elaine's thumbs in them as they usually did.

Elaine smiled. "People love seeing pictures of themselves online. That's most of it. It's not much of a gig—you'd be amazed at the number of gardens I'm photographing. Someone always has a prize zucchini or something. Here, I'll show you some."

She proceeded to take out her phone and flip through at least a dozen photos. There was Beulah Foster's 100th birthday at Greener Pastures. There was a retirement party for someone who'd been working at the same business for 40 years. And there was a children's birthday party with all the attendees lined up for a picture.

"Jack's in this one," said Elaine, pointing him out proudly.

"That's a big party," said Myrtle. "Birthday parties in my day were usually family only."

"Oh, they're big deals now. This one was at night. Jack had so much sugar that he was wired and didn't sleep a wink all night."

"He and Miles should hang out," said Myrtle dryly.

A minute later, Elaine hurried back out to run to the store. Myrtle and Jack sat down at the kitchen table and had their snack and lemonade while Jack regaled Myrtle with his tales from preschool. These were mostly about who was his favorite friend and who he liked to play with on the playground outside the church.

Then Myrtle showed Jack his surprise and his eyes lit up. Myrtle said, "See? The doors really open and the lights really go when you move the switch." She complimented herself on her generosity by making sure at the consignment shop that the ambulance either didn't have a siren or that the siren was non-functioning. She hadn't wanted to bother Red and Elaine . . . well, mostly Elaine. Although now she could see it might have been better to gift a loud toy that could potentially interrupt Elaine's creative process.

Jack and Myrtle played with the ambulance for a long time. They put toy superheroes in it and came up with scenarios where they had to go to the hospital, despite their special powers. Then Jack put toy cars in the ambulance to take *them* to the hospital. Jack provided the siren sounds for the missing ambulance siren, so that worked out well.

After a while, Jack started getting sleepy, much as Elaine predicted. Myrtle found a low-key children's show on TV and got Jack settled on the sofa with his favorite toy and a blanket. He rested his head sleepily on a cushy pillow.

That's when Myrtle's phone rang, which was perfect timing. She saw it was Wanda and walked into the kitchen where she could still keep an eye on Jack. "Hi, Wanda."

Wanda grated, "Hi there. Sorry about not answerin'. Took a nap."

"A nap? Is everything all right, Wanda? I don't remember your taking many naps during the day." Myrtle frowned. "This isn't still to do with Lillian's death, is it?"

Wanda sighed. The sigh graduated into a cough. She paused and then said, "Maybe. Kinda hard when bad things can't be stopped."

Myrtle said, "You stop bad things all the time with your column. If there was one person who was silly enough not to listen to your warning, she got what she deserved."

Wanda gave a reluctant chuckle. "Don't suffer fools lightly, do ya?"

"Not by half," agreed Myrtle. "And this is exactly why I called. I wanted to check in on you since you were so funny over Lillian's murder. I have a lot on my plate right now and absolutely *can-not* handle if something were to happen to you on top of it all. Got that?"

The grating chuckle again. "Yes, ma'am."

"All right, then. I'm glad that's settled. Do you need me to come up there? Help out? Bring a meal?" asked Myrtle.

"No, Dan's been right thoughtful lately."

"Well, that's amazing. I'm rather keeled over by that news, actually. Now onto something else, Wanda, while I have you on the phone," said Myrtle.

"Think the battery's dyin'," croaked Wanda.

"I'll be quick. For one, Sloan has agreed to give you a raise."

Wanda sounded pleased. "That's good."

"And one other matter before I let you go. Have you had any other . . . insights? Anything at all that might be helpful with this case?" asked Myrtle.

"Anger is powerful," said Wanda in a tired voice.

"Anger is. The only problem is *everyone* was angry at Lillian. Well, except for Rowan, perhaps. The caterer."

Wanda snorted. "Him's angriest of all. But hides it."

Myrtle raised her eyebrows. "So should I speak with him again, then?"

But the phone cut off, the waning battery finally dead.

Myrtle walked back into the living room where Jack was completely asleep, one hand on the ambulance, in front of the TV. She carefully turned the volume of the children's show down and settled into a chair with Elaine's writings.

Thirty minutes later, she called Miles. "It's dreadful, Miles. Really dreadful."

"What is?" asked Miles in a sleepy voice.

"Were you sleeping?" asked Myrtle suspiciously.

"Just a tiny catnap." Now he sounded wary.

"Well, try to wake up for a minute."

Miles said, "Wait, it's not time for supper, is it?"

"No, no, this is about something else. Elaine's newest hobby—her scribblings. Miles, they're really, really awful. What am I supposed to do?" asked Myrtle.

Miles said, "Tell her they're the best thing since baked bread. Just gloss over it."

"I'm not sure I know how to do that."

"Why don't you just edit them for typos and poor grammar? Then it looks as if you've put time and thought into reading and you can leave out any actual criticism," said Miles.

Myrtle said, "Yes, but Elaine actually proofread fairly well. There aren't any glaring errors. They're just bad, that's all."

Miles gave the verbal equivalent of a shrug. "I'm not sure, Myrtle. But I don't think it's your responsibility to be the gatekeeper. Let her send off some of her writing to publishers or contests and let *them* reject her. I'll see you for supper."

And Miles, apparently eager to get back to his nap, hung up.

Which is when Myrtle's doorbell rang. She glared at the front door. Now Elaine would be here to get Jack and she'd want to know Myrtle's opinion. Myrtle was used to giving only honest opinions and wasn't sure she could provide anything else. She sighed as she walked to the door.

When she opened it, she found Red there.

Chapter Fifteen

"Hi, Mama," he said in his booming voice.

She frowned at him. "Shh. Jack's asleep."

Red glanced over at the sofa. "Well, he's going to have to wake up anyway to go back home. I offered to pick him up for Elaine since I was closer." His gaze wandered to Myrtle's kitchen table and Elaine's folder. He grimaced. "It looks like you've been reading Elaine's stories."

Myrtle gave a solemn nod. "Yes."

Red said, "What did you think?"

Myrtle gave Red a look.

"Yep. That's about what I thought, too. I was hoping *one* of her hobbies would be something she'd have a little talent in. And she really likes this one," said Red.

Myrtle said, "Well, I can't tell her they're terrible. But I can't tell her they're great."

"You're just too blunt." Although there was a gleam of respect in his eyes when he said it.

Myrtle sighed. "Too many years of teaching, I suppose. I'll have to come up with something that will satisfy me to say and won't completely upset Elaine."

"I'm sure you'll be able to." Red walked over and picked Jack up in one swoop. Jack didn't even stir. He shook his head. "He's really out. I thought for sure he'd wake up when I picked him up. I've got to get going since I have another stop to make tonight."

"Do you?" asked Myrtle, sounding innocent.

"Just have to run by Tallulah Porter's house. She wanted to see me about something," said Red.

"Something to do with the case?" asked Myrtle, remembering Tallulah's desire to speak with Red at Lillian's funeral.

Red snorted. "Knowing Miz Porter, it'll have something more to do with neighborhood kids trampling through her yard or a problem with one of the neighbors being too loud at night. She's a complainer, that one."

"How's the case going?" asked Myrtle in a very offhanded way.

Red narrowed his eyes. "It's going just fine. Keep out of it, Mama."

Myrtle blinked at him. "I don't know what you're talking about."

"Everywhere I've gone lately and everyone I've spoken with in conjunction with the case has said the same thing: 'I've seen your mama today. She's looking so good!'" He looked sternly at Myrtle.

"Well, it's certainly nice to be told I'm looking good," said Myrtle complacently.

"The point is that you're very close to talking with all of the same people I'm talking to."

Myrtle said, "Only because Miles and I needed to deliver sympathy casseroles to Lillian's family. We were in garden club together, Red."

"And Rowan Blaine?" Red knit his eyebrows.

"Tippy wanted me to check on the catering for the garden club auction. You and Elaine have a conflict, correct? I haven't had your RSVP yet."

Red ignored the attempt to sidetrack him. "And Bianca Lloyd?"

"Someone had to make sure we were still getting our flower arrangements for the auction," said Myrtle, looking displeased. "Really, Red, you do go on and on."

He briefly closed his eyes. Then he said, "Do you need me to do some yard work for you?"

"I have Dusty for that."

"Yes, but clearly Dusty hasn't been by. The grass is getting pretty tall, even though we haven't had rain. And it's supposed to rain tonight. What's going on with Dusty?" asked Red.

"The same thing that's always going on with Dusty. Chronic laziness."

"I'll give him a call," said Red grimly. "I really don't have time to stop chasing down a murderer to tinker in my mother's yard. Especially around a large collection of gnomes."

Myrtle glared at him. "No, *I'll* call him. It's *my* yard. And if you didn't bulldoze into my business, there wouldn't *be* any gnomes out there."

Red shifted Jack and he again didn't stir. "Well, let me know if he isn't responsive. I need to get this little guy home . . . he's getting heavier by the second."

"Wait—you need to take his toy ambulance back with you."

Red held out his hand and Myrtle gestured to the large ambulance. He pulled his hand back. "I thought you meant an ambulance I could hold in my palm. That thing is as big as Jack!"

"It's fun-sized," said Myrtle, frowning. "Jack loves it. And the siren doesn't work, so it's a quiet toy."

"I'm sure he does love it, but I can't cart it back home right now with my hands full. I'll grab it later on in the week. Bye, Mama." He pushed his way out the door.

After Red left, Myrtle became engrossed in the book she was reading. So engrossed that she didn't notice what time it was until Pasha leapt through the window to rub against her and inquire about food.

"Heavens! It's late." She quickly put out cat food and called Miles on the phone.

"Mmm?" he sleepily answered.

"Miles! We're supposed to go to supper. If we wait any longer, it'll be breakfast time."

Miles grunted in alarm and there was commotion on the other end as he maneuvered himself to see a clock. Then he said dryly, "It's only eight. I think we're safe."

"Some of the places will close in an hour. I'm not in the mood to make myself something to eat at this point in the day," said Myrtle.

"I'll be right there."

Ten minutes later Miles was there, looking a bit rumpled and still half-asleep, but ready to go. He escorted Myrtle to the car.

"Where are we heading?" he asked as he backed out of the driveway.

"We're not exactly spoiled for choice, are we? Maybe the diner?"

Miles made a face. "Can we get something a little healthier?"

"Chinese?"

Miles glanced sideways at her.

"What? You could get vegetables and brown rice. That's not so bad," said Myrtle. She paused. "There's the fancy place that's just opened. They're sure to have healthy choices."

"Will they have fancy prices, though?" asked Miles. He knew Myrtle was on a budget.

"I can always get a salad," said Myrtle with a shrug. "And that's probably just as well. I should eat healthy tonight, too. Could you take a slight detour? Go past Tallulah's house?"

Miles frowned. "Not exactly a slight detour."

"I know. Red came by this afternoon to pick Jack up and mentioned he'd be speaking with Tallulah. I'm just curious as to what transpired."

"What transpired?" asked Miles. "Wasn't it just a conversation?"

"It might have been. Or maybe Tallulah confessed. In which case, she wouldn't have any lights on at her house and her car would be there. And she'd be at the police station and there'd likely be all sorts of state police cars at her house, gathering evidence to use against her," said Myrtle thoughtfully.

Miles made the detour.

When he drove to Tallulah's house, they couldn't even get close. There were tons of police cars, forensic units, and people.

They looked at each other.

"I guess she confessed," said Miles slowly.

Myrtle frowned. "Something about this doesn't make sense. Get a little closer."

"I can't get closer, Myrtle. There are vehicles on both sides of the street."

"Pull into Lillian's driveway. We know *she's* not there."

Miles looked uncomfortable. "Perhaps her children are there."

"Martin has a mansion and is most likely choosing to hang out there instead of in Lillian's modest house. And Annie was practically allergic to Lillian. I don't think she's there."

Miles crept forward until he got to Lillian's driveway. He popped into it.

Myrtle took off her seatbelt and sat forward on her seat. Her eyes narrowed at the forensics team going by. "Miles, I don't think Tallulah confessed. I think Tallulah's dead."

"Look, there's Red." Miles gestured at him. Then he grimaced. "He's coming over."

Myrtle muttered, "Look at him. He's had a rough night. He's all sweaty and irritable-looking."

"He's frequently irritable-looking."

"Yes, but this is worse. He's very unsettled. This will be the best time to get information from him," said Myrtle.

Red walked up to the car and Miles reluctantly put the window down. Red said, "Mama, I'm not at all surprised to see you here. But Miles?"

Miles reddened. "Your mother is very persuasive."

"Is the whole town talking about this or is this a coincidence that you're here?" asked Red.

Myrtle said, "I haven't heard a word about it. Miles and I were just taking the scenic route on our way to supper." She paused. "She's dead, isn't she? Tallulah."

Chapter Sixteen

Red rubbed his eyes. "She sure is."

"She didn't have the opportunity to speak with you, then?" asked Myrtle.

"She did not." Red looked very tired.

It occurred to Myrtle that Red hadn't discovered a single body in all the murders he'd investigated. Discovering this one seemed to have really shaken him up.

Miles said, "Were you able to just walk in? Her door was unlocked?" He colored a little. "Sorry for the nosiness. It just reminded me of the way it was with Lillian when I found her."

Red nodded. "It was slightly ajar and Tallulah didn't answer when I called her name. Sort of worried me since she'd been so eager to talk to me and I was punctual. So I walked inside." He frowned. "Mama, did you know her at all?"

"Just a bit."

"Was she a golfer?" asked Red.

Myrtle nodded. "She certainly was. Apparently, quite a good one." Her eyes narrowed. "Was Tallulah killed with a golf club?"

Red sighed.

Myrtle said, "Well, this murderer certainly seems to arrive at homes unprepared. He always seems to grab whatever is around as a weapon."

Red was quiet. Then he said, "I wish we could figure out what was behind all this."

Myrtle was pleased by his inclusive choice of pronoun. "Anger."

Red raised his eyebrows.

"Anger is behind it." Myrtle nodded her head sagely. She knew better than to tell Red where that little insight had come from. Red never seemed to take Wanda's statements very seriously. To his detriment.

"Unfortunately," he said tiredly, "we have lots of angry people involved with this case." He glanced over at the house where the state police were busily going in and out. "Mama, you don't have any idea what Tallulah was so eager to speak to me about, do you?"

Myrtle wished she did. She would have loved to produce some game-changing information at this point. Instead, she shook her head. "No. Only that I could tell it was something weighing on her mind. When I saw her at Lillian's funeral, she was watching you anxiously to see if you had a free moment to talk."

Red groaned. "And I was totally tied up with the woman worried about truancy."

"Exactly. Then you had to rush away," said Myrtle.

Miles cleared his throat. "I thought perhaps she might be wanting to confess to the crime. That she had a guilty conscience."

Myrtle shot him a look at *his* choice of pronoun. It had been what *they'd* thought.

Red said with a short laugh. "Good guess, except that clearly wasn't the case. She must have known something that someone else didn't want getting out." He glanced again at the state police. "All right, I should get going. And you should, too," he said sternly. "You're trespassing, after all."

"Simply getting out of the way of the official vehicles," said Myrtle breezily. "We'll leave soon. We're heading to dinner."

Red looked wistful at the mention of dinner before striding off to join the other cops.

Miles looked in his rear-view mirror and his eyes opened wide. "Annie is pulling into the driveway!"

"Well, she's not going to have us arrested for trespassing, Miles, for heaven's sake. And there's plenty of room for her car because you pulled so carefully to the side. Maybe she'll even have some information for us," said Myrtle.

Annie gave them a brief smile before staring for a few moments at the house next-door. She walked over to their car.

"Sorry we're in your driveway," said Myrtle. "I wanted to speak with Red to see what was going on and there was no room on the street."

Annie said distractedly, "No, that's fine. This driveway is usually deserted now, anyway. I'm just here to start organizing Mama's things. What *is* going on at Tallulah's?"

Myrtle told her. Then she said, "So you weren't here earlier, dear? Organizing your mother's things? Such a pity, since you might have seen something."

Annie shook her head. "No, I was busy earlier at home. I needed to clean up and organize at my own house before coming over here, otherwise I'd have been too tired coming home. Martin is not going to be any help at all," she said with a sigh. "So I didn't see anything. Don't know anything. And why would anyone murder Tallulah? It seems crazy. Are they systematically taking out everyone on the street?"

Myrtle said, "We think Tallulah must have seen something that might have exposed your mother's killer."

Annie slumped a little. "This is all so incredible. I mean, I'm leaving Bradley because it's a town where nothing *happens*. And suddenly, things are happening here all the time. Bad things." She paused. "And now I'm even wondering if I really want to leave at all. After all, Mama is gone and she's the main reason I was looking to leave in the first place."

Myrtle gave her a sympathetic look. "Family relationships can be tricky, can't they?"

A single tear trickled down Annie's face. To Myrtle's relief, no others seemed tempted to follow. In a somewhat shaky voice, Annie said, "Yes. I've been feeling bad about Mama's death, mostly because it's made life so much easier for me. Mama would berate me all the time. I could never seem to do anything right. She never liked a single decision I ever made, nothing I did in school was ever good enough. It was one thing after another."

Myrtle made a tsking sound. "That's dreadfully unfair to you, Annie. She was too harsh."

"And very controlling. But that's the funny thing about being controlled. After you aren't anymore, it's a huge adjustment. I've had to really stop and think what I need to do next. Right now, I'm just taking baby steps like cleaning out Mama's house. But soon I'll have to figure out the bigger picture."

Myrtle said slowly, "There was *one* thing I wanted to ask you about, Annie. You'd mentioned you'd been watching *Tomorrow's Promise* at the time your mother died."

"That's right. Well, I guess we don't really know exactly when she died, but that's what I was doing that evening. I was just trying to chill out after a long day." Annie's tone changed and she sounded cautious as she spoke. "One of my grandmothers got me hooked on the show when I was a teenager."

Myrtle nodded. "It's just that I happen to be something of an expert when it comes to *Tomorrow's Promise*. I've been watching for decades. And I could tell when I spoke with you about it that you clearly haven't been watching the latest episodes."

Annie slumped. "Got it." For a moment, it looked as if she was searching her mind for an appropriate alibi. Then she sighed. "It's true. I wasn't at home that night. Not that I had anyone to confirm I was home anyway. The truth is that I was out driving. Sometimes I like to go out to the public beach area of the lake and sit and just look at the moon and stars for a while. It helps me get centered again. And, of course, I went past Mama's house a couple of times when I did. When Red asked me, I just panicked and *Tomorrow's Promise* was the first thing to come to mind. But I promise I had nothing to do with Mama's death . . . *or* Tallulah's."

Annie glanced again over at Tallulah's house. "Now I feel bad that I even thought she might be involved in Mama's death."

Myrtle said, "It's only natural for you to speculate about it. And considering what you told me about the pending real estate transaction, it made sense that Tallulah might have been angry enough to confront your mother."

"And now it looks like Tallulah didn't have anything to do with Mama's murder at all. In fact, she might have even known who did it. Now we'll never know. This has all been so frustrating. I hope Red can get to the bottom of things." She sighed again. "I suppose I should go in and start sorting things. I'm not even sure where to start."

"Clothing might be easiest, although it's the most personal," said Myrtle.

Annie nodded. "It sure would be a lot easier if Martin thought to come over and help me with it." A tone of discontent edged into her voice. "His mind is totally focused on getting money from Mama's will."

Myrtle asked delicately, "Is he having some financial struggles, then?"

Annie snorted. "Struggles? He's drowning. Martin seems to fancy himself a big spender, so he has the big house and the expensive car. His wardrobe probably costs five times what mine does. And he hawks insurance."

Myrtle said, "I'm surprised he was able to get loans if his income wouldn't support his lifestyle."

Annie said, "Well, you have banks that are eager to make loans. And he *did* have cash for a while. I happen to know he gambled. For a while, he was winning, too. But then he started to lose and the more he lost, the more he gambled to try and get his money back." She made a face. "Not a smart tactic." She glanced at the house. "All right, I'm off. See you soon."

She trudged off to Lillian's house, looking as if she had the weight of the world on her shoulders.

Myrtle said thoughtfully, "It sure sounds like a cash infusion would have been very helpful for Martin."

Miles said, "Yes, but how much money are we talking about for Lillian's estate? It seems like a rather modest business to me."

Myrtle looked across at Tallulah's again and narrowed her eyes. "For heaven's sake. Red is on his way over to shoo us off again. Doesn't he have better things to do?"

"I don't think that's what he's doing," said Miles slowly. "Look, he's heading to his cruiser."

Sure enough, Red was striding rapidly to his police car, not over to speak with them.

Myrtle raised her eyebrows. "And Perkins is getting in the car with him! They both seem very grim. Let's follow them."

Miles gloomily looked at his watch. "The restaurants will be closing soon. I'm getting pretty hungry."

"We'll have food at my house once we figure out what's going on. Let's go, Miles!" said Myrtle impatiently as Miles slowly started up the engine and cautiously backed out of Lillian's driveway.

Red and Perkins disappeared around a corner. "Step on it!" said Myrtle wildly.

Miles gripped the steering wheel. "I'm going over the speed limit."

"Barely!"

"I've caught up with them," said Miles in a relieved voice.

"I think they're heading to Martin's house," said Myrtle, leaning forward until her seatbelt pulled her back a bit. "There's nowhere else they could be going."

A minute later, she was proven right as Red's police cruiser turned down Martin's long driveway.

"Hold on. Let's wait a second and let them get inside the house first," said Myrtle. "Otherwise, Red will shut me down before we even get to the front door."

Miles looked uneasy. "Won't we be interrupting official police business?"

"Well, of *course* we will be. That's the whole point. Just park right here until they walk in Martin's house."

Miles continued, "I don't think Red will be happy to see us."

"Naturally. But he isn't going to arrest us. All we're doing is checking in on Martin about the silent auction," said Myrtle.

Miles said, "But we've already done that. He said it was fine for the auction to proceed."

"We'll just say it's garden club business. We'll be vague."

"If I'd known what garden club membership entailed, I'd never have joined," grumbled Miles.

Myrtle said impatiently, "This isn't complicated. I could simply say I wanted to give Martin a preview of the tribute we're giving to Lillian. The point is that we need to figure out what's going on."

Miles looked unhappily at the large house.

"Okay, they're in. Let's go," said Myrtle.

When they reached the front door, Myrtle turned the doorknob.

Miles gasped. "We should ring the doorbell, Myrtle."

"Why? Clearly Martin is otherwise engaged right now. He may not be able to answer it." Myrtle walked inside. "Yoo-hoo! Martin? It's Myrtle."

There was a loud groan from the living room. Myrtle hurried in that direction with Miles miserably following her.

They found Perkins, who rose politely in greeting; Red, whose face was furious; and Martin, who looked rather ill.

"Oh, goodness!" said Myrtle in an overly innocent tone. "Are we interrupting something?"

Red looked at the ceiling. "Yes, you are. As you well know."

"Miles and I are simply here on garden club business," said Myrtle with a sniff.

Miles gave Red a weak smile.

Red said, "It doesn't really matter because we're going to continue our conversation down at the station. Since someone hasn't been forthcoming."

He and Perkins stood up and Martin turned white. He spread his hands out in supplication. "Look, I don't know what you want from me. I don't know that wretched woman at all! Tallulah was just my mother's next-door neighbor. I never even had a conversation with her. Well, except to try to sell her insurance. Besides that? Never."

Perkins said coldly, "Then it's even more interesting that we found something of yours at the crime scene a few minutes ago."

Martin blinked at him, looking startled. Then his expression grew angry. "My business card holder, maybe? Because it's missing. Somebody is setting me up!"

"Now who would want to do that?" asked Red.

Martin was now gesticulating even more. "My sister, for one! She's never liked me. Annie was always jealous of my relationship with our mother. Besides, if I'm in jail, she can use Mama's inheritance to get out of town."

Red said, "Well, she couldn't allow you to profit from your crime, could she?"

"It wasn't my crime! Okay, if it wasn't Annie who set me up, it could have been a ton of other people. Your suspects, whoever they are. The killer would try to set me up to deflect attention from himself. Come on, you know that's how it works! Like I said, I've never even been over to that house." Martin's voice was getting louder and shriller.

Red drawled, "Someone spotted you at your mother's today."

"There's a huge difference between being at my mother's house and being at Tallulah's. I never said I'd never been at *Mama's* house," spat Martin.

Perkins said in a clipped voice, "It's interesting that you were at your mother's *today*. Your sister told us you haven't been over there much. It would be very easy to dash over to Tallulah Porter's house and murder her."

"For what reason?" Martin gave a disbelieving laugh.

"Perhaps she saw you the night of your mother's death. Maybe she was planning on telling the police what she saw," said Perkins.

"Maybe you're just desperate and trying to find your killer. But it isn't me. I can tell you exactly why I was at my mother's house today. Annie said she was going over there to start clearing Mama's things out. I didn't want to help her, but I didn't want her to get rid of some of the stuff I wanted. I ran over there and threw a few things I liked in the car," said Martin. "That's *it*. End of story."

Red asked, "You didn't see anything suspicious next door while you were there?"

"I couldn't have been less interested in what was going on next door," said Martin.

Perkins said, "Unfortunately, we still have evidence you were there. We're going to need to bring you in."

Martin's voice was shrill again. "Why on earth would I have wanted to kill my mother? I actually got along with her pretty well."

"We know about your debts. We know you argued with your mother about money," said Red.

"I need a lawyer," said Martin furiously.

"We'll be sure to get you one when we get to the station," said Red. He turned a stern gaze on Myrtle and Miles. "Your garden club business is going to have to wait."

Myrtle and Miles walked back to the car, watching as Red ushered Martin into the backseat of his police cruiser.

Miles said, "Well, that was interesting. I was rather pulling for Martin to be innocent, since he was such a reader. I usually don't think of ardent readers as being especially violent."

Myrtle shook her head. "I don't think he did it."

Miles said, "But the evidence seems to indicate otherwise."

"Evidence can be faked, just like he said. He was probably set-up."

Miles said, "I don't know, Myrtle. I remember him playing around with that business card case. I think it was one of those things he liked to fidget with. He took it over to Tallulah's to see what she had to say and was fidgeting with it there and dropped it or set it down at some point. Then he killed her, apparently with a golf club, and left in a panic."

"And you think he killed his mother."

Miles shrugged. "He'd argued with her. He was clearly in debt and needed money. Maybe Lillian had finally seen him for what he was and denied him more cash. He was desperate and angry and acted impetuously."

"Hitting her over the head with a dog's feeding station." Myrtle quirked her eyebrows.

"It was the closest thing at hand."

Myrtle tilted her head to one side, considering this. "I just don't know. There's a weakness to Martin that doesn't really translate to murder. Maybe he did. But it just seems unlikely to me."

"Maybe it was planned then and *not* impetuous. He realized he'd be inheriting money from his mother and he killed her when her back was turned," said Miles.

"That's even worse than if he'd acted out of desperation. Besides, I think you're right—Lillian wasn't a wealthy woman. She definitely was comfortable, but I don't think it was enough money to kill over."

Miles pulled up to the restaurant. He sadly said, "They've already turned off the 'open' sign."

Myrtle snorted. "This town closes up ridiculously early during the week."

"The diner was already closed, too. I saw it when we passed by," said Miles morosely.

"Well, there are two options. We can go to the all-night breakfast place out near the highway or we can go to my house and I can make us something."

Miles's expression revealed that neither of these options was particularly attractive. "There's a third option. We could go to *my* house. I happen to have some food there I could prepare."

Myrtle looked at him in surprise. "Now that sounds nice! If we run by my house first, I can grab my laptop and work on my Tallulah story for Sloan while you cook."

"I think the paper's already printed for tonight, isn't it?"

"Most certainly. But Sloan will have it first thing tomorrow and will have plenty of time to design the rest of the paper around my article," said Myrtle in a satisfied voice.

Chapter Seventeen

The next morning, Myrtle called Tippy. "How is the auction coming together?"

Tippy sounded a bit distracted. "I was so organized with it. But suddenly, there are a million things to do." Her voice turned hopeful. "You don't happen to know what Miles's day looks like today, do you? We could use a bit of muscle."

Myrtle crossed her fingers and said, "I happen to know Miles has nothing important on his schedule later today. He and I would love to come over to the venue and help set up." She paused. "Do you know when the caterer and florist will be arriving? Maybe that would be a good time for us to be there."

Tippy said, "Bianca will be here with the flowers around 5:00. Rowan should be here with the food around the same time. And thanks, Myrtle. You've been a real lifesaver for this event. Thank Miles for me, too."

Myrtle hung up the phone and beamed. She immediately called Miles. "We have a plan for the day."

"I thought we already *had* a plan for the day. The silent auction is at 6:30 this evening, right?" Miles's voice did not reflect enthusiasm for the auction.

"Yes, but Tippy needs more help. She said she needed muscle."

Miles groaned. "I never should have joined this club. What kind of muscles do they think I have? I worked in an office my entire life."

"Apparently, they think your muscles are better developed than their own, a notion I entirely agree with. Besides, it will give us an opportunity to speak with Rowan and Bianca. They'll both be there around 5:00 to set up."

Miles said, "They'll be busy with their food and flowers. They won't want to speak with us."

"I think they will. After all, we know more about Tallulah's death than almost anybody. They must be curious. I think they'll make time to talk to us."

"All right." Miles's voice was defeated. "But let's have a quiet day up until that point. I want to work my crossword and read the new book Carolyn found for me. And gather my strength for whatever show of power is required of me this evening."

Miles may have had a quiet day until they left for the auction. But Myrtle was a whirlwind of activity and restlessness. Because she was stuck at home, she took a walk. Pasha spotted her and walked along with her, glaring at neighbors who considered coming up to chat with Myrtle. When they got back home, Myrtle fed the feral cat. She promptly gobbled up the cat food, took a vigorous bath, and then fell into a deep sleep.

While Pasha slept, Myrtle thought she'd read her book. But as she read, she kept glancing around her living room and noticing dust, dust bunnies under the furniture, and the fact the entire room could use a good vacuuming. A vacuuming that had been interrupted the last time. That Puddin. She picked up her phone and proceeded to have another annoying conversation with Puddin. By the end of it, however, Puddin had reluctantly acquiesced to coming over to clean the following day.

Then Elaine called as soon as Myrtle had hung up the phone.

"Thanks again for watching Jack for me. I got *so* much done while he was there."

"It was no trouble at all. He was a perfect angel, the way he always is." Myrtle said this rather smugly. Jack was *always* very good with her, but she was aware this wasn't always the case for Elaine.

"Do you have a minute? I know the auction is tonight."

"I'm actually at loose ends right now, as a matter of fact."

"Did you have a chance to read my stories?" asked Elaine eagerly.

Myrtle had been considering her answer to this question. She didn't like to lie. "Elaine, the stories were edited *perfectly*. You did a remarkable job. I didn't see a single typo." This was the truth.

Elaine sounded pleased. "Wow, that's amazing! Especially since I know you pull out your red pen and use it on the newspaper all the time."

"You should offer editing services to Sloan," said Myrtle, completely genuinely. "Heaven knows he could use the help and you obviously have an excellent eye."

"It's only because I do a lot of reading," said Elaine modestly.

"Readers make the best editors."

Elaine said, "But what did you think of the *content* of the stories? Did you like them?"

Myrtle remembered Red had wanted her to discourage Elaine. She also remembered Red's pushiness and the fact he hadn't been very polite to her at Martin's house when he was arrested last night. She had the perfect answer for Elaine.

"Your stories showed excellent sense of mood. They reminded me quite a bit of Emily Brontë, to be completely honest."

Elaine gasped with pleasure. She had no way of knowing Myrtle loathed Emily Brontë's work.

"Thank you, Myrtle. You've made my day," gushed Elaine.

Myrtle said, "Do you know what you plan on doing with the stories? Are you submitting them to literary magazines? Anthologies? Publishers?" Myrtle crossed her fingers. She hoped the answer to this was no. Rejection was never fun and she had the feeling it might be crushing for someone like Elaine.

Elaine said, "At first, that's exactly what I thought I'd do. I wanted to share my stories with everybody! I even tried to get Sloan to add a section in the paper for literature."

Myrtle said cautiously, "How did that go over?"

Elaine laughed. "Not well. Apparently, Sloan doesn't think Bradley has a lot of literature lovers."

"He's probably right about that," said Myrtle with relief.

"Anyway, I looked into querying publishers, anthologies, contests, and magazines. It's a lot of work. I decided maybe I like writing for myself, most of all. It's cathartic, you know? So I'll keep them to myself."

"I can completely understand that," said Myrtle sincerely.

"And from time to time I might share a favorite with Red and you."

Myrtle winced. "Of course you will. Thank you, dear. I'll look forward to it." She paused. "On a completely different subject, how is Red doing? He seemed rather shaken up last night after finding Tallulah."

"He was. Do you know he's never discovered a single murder victim before? He seemed much better this morning when he left to go to work, though. Even though I don't think he slept very well. Poor Tallulah." Jack started yelling in the background and Elaine quickly said, "Better run. Hope you have fun at the auction tonight."

Later that afternoon, Miles and Myrtle headed off to the auction to help set up.

"I'm not sure a suit was the best choice of attire, Miles."

Miles said, "It's a dressy event. I'm wearing what the invitation stated."

"Yes, but now you have to lug things around and perspire in your suit," said Myrtle.

"You're dressed up, too." Miles glanced over at Myrtle in the passenger seat.

"I'm wearing my funeral outfit, recently laundered, and nothing very fancy. And I *won't* be perspiring. I plan on speaking with Bianca and Rowan under cover of making sure everything is correct." Myrtle smoothed down a small wrinkle in her funeral outfit.

Miles raised his eyebrows. "Won't Tippy think you're slacking off? She seems to think you're going to be helping set up the event . . . whatever that entails."

"Tippy is just grateful to see me at all," said Myrtle breezily. "I volunteered to be there—I don't *have* to be there. I've already helped her out with the arrangements a couple of times. And Tippy wouldn't dream of fussing at a woman old enough to be her mother."

Miles nodded. "You're right. I can't imagine Tippy doing that."

"Besides, setting up this event in this venue takes a certain amount of magic. The place is incredibly pedestrian. It has low tile ceilings, dark wood paneling, and a polished concrete floor. Tippy might be stringing lights everywhere. Octogenarians do not string lights."

Miles said, "I'm not sure my age group strings lights either."

"Then hang out close to me. You might be able to escape it."

When Miles pulled up to the venue, Bianca was just starting to pull arrangements out of her car.

Myrtle waved to her. "Miles can help!"

Miles shot her a baleful look.

Bianca flushed and said gratefully, "Would you? There are a few of them. The vases are kind of heavy and it was going to take me forever."

Miles took one of the larger arrangements and headed for the building.

Myrtle said vaguely, "If you have something *small*, I could take it in." It was the kind of offer that wasn't supposed to be taken up on.

"Could you just bring my purse in? That would be a huge help," said Bianca.

A few minutes later, they were inside the building. Miles had set the arrangement down on the closest available surface since it *had* been quite heavy and Bianca showed him where it actually went.

Myrtle watched her work for a moment. Bianca was relaxed and professional, upbeat and confident. Myrtle said, "You seem very, very capable, Bianca. Isn't this your first event on your own?"

Bianca gave her a smile. "It sure is. I don't know but I feel suddenly like I've done a good job. Like I'm *excited* to show off the work I've done with the flowers. Is that weird? I should probably feel the total opposite since it's my first solo event."

Myrtle looked at her shrewdly. "Maybe it's because Lillian isn't here, overseeing you. I know she was a hard taskmaster."

Bianca thought about this for a moment. "You're right. I'd mess stuff up because Lillian totally expected me to mess stuff up. Here, everybody is expecting the flowers to look great and the flowers look great."

Myrtle watched Bianca rearrange some of the flowers and then said, "Did you hear about Lillian's neighbor? Tallulah?"

Bianca's face fell. "Somebody who came into the shop told me. She lived down the street from Lillian? I mean, do the police think somebody is targeting people in that neighborhood?"

"She lived directly next door to Lillian. And no, I think this is much more personal than someone just randomly targeting people on the same street."

Bianca looked grim. "It's terrible, no matter what. I didn't know her at all. Lillian one time mentioned her, but she didn't say much. Like I said, she didn't talk about personal stuff a lot. It happened at night?"

Myrtle nodded. "Well, after dark, anyway."

"That's so scary. I mean, that's always when I'm at home alone with my little boy. I'm planning on getting another lock for my door because now I just don't feel safe." She watched as Rowan asked one of his staff to rearrange a chaffing dish. "He seems happier today, too. Maybe it's just easier when Lillian isn't here." Then she looked really guilty. "I feel awful for saying that."

"What exactly transpired between Rowan Blaine and Lillian? I understand they might not have been getting along," said Myrtle.

Bianca paused and said miserably, "I wasn't supposed to talk about it."

"I don't think it matters to Lillian now," said Myrtle briskly.

Bianca looked around her as if the set-up crew was determined to listen in. She said in a low voice, "Lillian didn't get along with Rowan at all. They were both the same kind of people. Perfectionists, I guess? Anyway, Rowan made Lillian mad because he'd always recommend this other florist to people for their events."

Myrtle frowned. "I didn't think there *was* another florist."

"There isn't here in Bradley, but there's one in Iva. It made Lillian really upset. He said her arrangements were really simplistic. Something like that." Bianca looked uncomfortable.

Myrtle said, "Did Lillian tell Rowan what she thought? Because I can't imagine her keeping her anger to herself."

"She kept it to herself. But she launched this . . . sort of campaign against him." Bianca flushed. She clamped her lips together as if she wanted to keep from talking about her former employer.

Myrtle sighed. "Bianca, I promise you, there's absolutely nothing Lillian can do to hurt you now. And who knows? What you tell me could end up being very useful for solving this case. Maybe we can figure out who did this to Lillian. But you have to tell me what you know."

Bianca reluctantly continued. "Well, like I said, Lillian didn't talk to me much about personal stuff. But the shop isn't very big and her voice would carry when she was on the phone or when she was talking to a customer up front and I was in the back room. I heard her spreading all kinds of gossip about Rowan right after that."

"What kinds of rumors?" asked Myrtle.

"It was stuff about his business; that his business was overstretched and he was about to go under. That he wasn't fulfilling what his customers asked for. That the events were sloppy. Just really negative gossip." Bianca looked miserable.

"And you think this is because Rowan was sending business to another florist?"

Bianca nodded. "That, and the fact he'd also gossip about Lillian. I guess she thought she was getting him back. But there wasn't any truth to it, I know—Rowan's business is real successful. She was just trying to get him back, that's all."

Myrtle said, "I suppose you must have heard about Martin, too."

Bianca looked worried. "I did. I wondered what would happen to the shop if he stayed in jail." She shook her head. "Selfish, I know. But that's the kind of thing I think about now. I have to keep caring for Tim." She paused. "I'd better finish up with this stuff before people start coming in." She hurried away.

Myrtle looked around for Miles. Tippy had gotten hold of him and he was moving tables around, still wearing his suit jacket. Myrtle sighed.

A dulcet voice came from behind her. "Don't you look nice tonight?"

Chapter Eighteen

She turned to see Rowan there and smiled. "Thank you, Rowan. This is technically my funeral outfit, but I decided it should have other purposes."

He tilted his head to assess the ensemble. Then he slowly nodded. "There is absolutely no reason to limit that outfit to the realm of funeral services. It suits you well." He added in a low voice, "As long as it's not bad luck! Wouldn't that be horrible? If we had yet *another* grisly death in Bradley?"

Myrtle said crisply, "Perish the thought! Two is more than enough."

Rowan leaned in a little closer. "What do you think about Martin's arrest?"

Myrtle asked, "What do *you* think about it?"

Rowan said, "I'm completely shocked. I mean, totally shocked through and through. If there was one thing I thought was obvious, it's that Martin loved his mother very much. He always spoke of her in such fond terms. He seemed so devastated by her death." Rowan frowned. "I do hope this isn't going to hold up any remuneration I'm owed for the funeral reception. Wouldn't that be awful?"

Myrtle said, "I suppose we'll have to see. I'm not convinced Martin had anything to do with his mother's death."

Rowan's eyes opened wide. "But I hear there was evidence. I mean, there was evidence at Tallulah's house that implicated Martin. That's the scuttlebutt, anyway."

Rowan was the sort of person who knew everything going on in a town. How he knew about police evidence, though, was unclear.

Myrtle shrugged. "Maybe there's evidence, maybe not. Martin says he wasn't there." She knew Rowan would be spreading the information all over town. Maybe Martin would still be able to live and work in Bradley when he left the jail if Rowan spread an alternate version of events.

Rowan's eyes bugged out. "Really? Well, you're the mother of the police chief, so I'll take your word for it. I suppose evidence can also be faked, can't it?"

Bianca walked by then and looked at them curiously. Rowan waved a cheery hand and as soon as Bianca passed by, he said, "That poor girl. Do you know how absolutely awful Lillian was to her? She acted as if Bianca was some sort of half-wit or something. Terrible, terrible behavior."

Myrtle clucked over this and then innocently added, "I heard Lillian wasn't too kind to you, either, some of the time."

Rowan blinked at her and then burst into laughter. "Red should take you on as his partner, Miss Myrtle. Oh my goodness, how *do* you find your information?"

Bianca again passed curiously by and Rowan waited until she was out of earshot again. "I can tell you Lillian wasn't fun to work with. She wasn't just a perfectionist with her own staff; she

was a perfectionist with mine, as well. When she started carp-
ing at one of my employees, I'd really had enough. Only *I* am
allowed to fuss at my staff and they hadn't done anything fuss-
worthy. So I started recommending a competing florist in Iva to
folks who were putting on events."

"But not for this one," said Myrtle.

"Oh, no. No, because Lillian was a member of the garden
club so of course they needed to use her shop for the flowers.
Lillian would never have forgiven them, otherwise."

Myrtle said, "I take it Lillian didn't appreciate having business go elsewhere. Did she know why it happened?"

Rowan nodded. "She was a smart cookie. She figured out I'd
been the one who'd sent people to other florists."

"And she retaliated," said Myrtle.

"Absolutely! She was positively vicious. Livid."

Myrtle said, "She approached you about it? Argued with
you?"

A cagey look crossed Rowan's handsome features. "Lillian
did something else. She started rumors about the stability of my
catering business. An argument would have been much better.
She told people I was in financial disarray and wasn't following
through on events the way I was supposed to. Really vile stuff."
He paused. "You probably have some influence over Red, don't
you?"

"I'm not sure about that," said Myrtle dryly.

"Maybe you could tell him there's no way I could murder
anyone. I really don't know him very well, being a law-abiding
citizen and all. But for some reason, Red has been speaking to
me a lot. He seems to think I'm a likely suspect. And if Martin

really wasn't responsible for these deaths, I'm sure Red will be by again. It's not very good for business to have a cop parked outside all the time."

Myrtle asked, "Why don't you just give him your alibi for Tallulah's death? He won't consider you as a suspect if it's impossible for you to have done it."

Rowan made a face. "That's just it—I wasn't doing anything remarkable whenever Tallulah was murdered. It was night-ish, wasn't it? It would have been so much better if I'd been at a large party making a fool of myself and everyone had seen me there. I'm not sure what I was doing, but I certainly wasn't out murdering Tallulah!"

"You knew her then?" asked Myrtle curiously. "Somehow I wouldn't have thought you two would have run in the same circles."

She watched as Miles staggered by, lugging a couple of chairs.

"We played golf sometimes on Saturdays," said Rowan. "I'm not much of a golfer, but Tallulah was a very forgiving friend. I'd never have laid a hand on her. Whatever I *was* doing was very boring. I was likely working in my office, doing payroll, budgeting, that type of thing. If it was a long stretch of desk work, I probably was on my treadmill. I have one of those space-saving ones that folds up in a jiffy when you don't need it out. I love that thing."

He continued, "You know, I couldn't really see Martin killing Lillian, either, now that you mention it. Extorting money? Yes. *Stealing* money? Perhaps. But murdering two people? I just can't imagine it. I mean, poor Tallulah! And of course I feel badly that Lillian was taken before her time. Her flowers were always lovely and she always did an exceptional job at everything she set out to do. But I didn't like the way she treated her family or her staff . . . or me."

Rowan glanced across the room and shuddered. "Heavens! Erma Sherman is heading this way. We should both make haste." But before he scurried away, he held her arm and said, "Any word on that business profile yet?"

Myrtle said, "Rats. I meant to ask Sloan about it yesterday and then my day got away from me. Don't worry; I'm writing the story and Sloan always lets me publish whatever I want to."

Rowan beamed. "Perfect. I just had new headshots done and I'm sure they'd look amazing in the piece! Better run." He scurried away.

Myrtle scurried away too, catching up with Miles who was now moving a lectern to a different location. He gave her a sour look.

Myrtle walked a bit closer to Tippy, who was frowning at a list she was holding.

"Everything seems to be going like clockwork," said Myrtle.

Tippy said absently, "Is it? I was going to say exactly the opposite." She sighed. "At least the food and flowers are basically set up. But then, everything is going quicker without Rowan and Lillian arguing." Her eyes opened wide and she clapped her hand over her mouth. "What an awful thing to say. Pardon me."

Myrtle said, "It's fine, Tippy. I understood the two of them didn't get along well. Had you seen them arguing lately?"

Tippy removed the hand from her mouth and sighed. "Just last week, not long before Lillian's death. Those two were like oil and water."

Myrtle made a show of gaping at the clock on the wall. "Oh, goodness! Is that the time? Tippy, I'm going to have to borrow Miles. I'd forgotten I'd offered to help Elaine with something and I need him to drive me over."

Tippy pursed her lips. "But you'll be back in time for the auction?"

"I wouldn't miss it for the world," said Myrtle. She waved over at Miles who hurried to join her as she walked out of the building.

"I hoped to be rescued a little earlier than that," said Miles.

"Better late than never," said Myrtle. "I did just hear something interesting from Tippy."

Miles said, "I hope it was high praise for my ability to move furniture around while wearing a suit."

"No, although I'm positive she was *thinking* it, Miles. No, Tippy said Rowan and Lillian had been arguing shortly before her death."

Miles said, "We'd heard earlier that they didn't get along. Sounds like more of the same."

"Except Rowan told us he hadn't seen Lillian for weeks," said Myrtle.

Miles looked impressed. "Good point. But then, Rowan seems clever enough to try to cover up the fact he had an argument with someone who soon became a murder victim."

They reached the car and Miles fumbled in his pocket for the keys. Myrtle said, "Now we need to figure out how to kill the next hour."

"While all dressed up," said Miles, looking down at his suit.

"We could go to the diner," said Myrtle.

Miles said, "It will look as if we've escaped from prom."

Myrtle shrugged. "If anyone asks, we can direct them to the silent auction. We'll be advertisements for the event."

"Won't whatever Rowan's cooking be a lot better than eating pimento cheese chili dogs at Bo's Diner?"

Myrtle said, "Who says we can't have both?"

Miles reached in his pocket and pulled out an antacid. "I had a feeling I should keep these handy."

A little over an hour later, they returned to the silent auction. Miles raised his eyebrows. "There are actually a lot of people here."

"Of course! People like to win things," said Myrtle.

Miles's eyebrows drew together as he looked over the baskets. "They actually are using Lillian's donation?" He looked somewhat horrified.

Myrtle studied the basket and said in a hushed voice, "It's not as if the feeding station is there. Nothing else was touched and obviously the family didn't want the stuff. I guess Tippy must have asked Martin and Annie what they wanted to do with it. I'm sure they just wanted it out of the way—one less thing they'd have to sort through."

By the end of the evening, Myrtle was feeling tired and grumpy and ready to go home. She'd had to avoid Erma Sherman five or six times and always by the skin of her teeth. The food had been very good, but she'd been a bit too enthusiastic in her ordering at the diner and was now totally stuffed. Miles was looking drowsy again and she wanted to escape from the auction before her driver was too sleepy to get her home safely. The only good part of the evening was her donation of the downtown Bradley drawing had sold.

She turned and saw Bianca beside her, giving her a shy smile.

"Goodness," said Myrtle. "I thought you'd be long gone."

"Oh, I just came back to pick up the arrangements after the auction wraps up. Tippy wanted to donate them to the retirement home, so I'm going to drop them by there."

Myrtle said, "That's a good idea." She paused as Bianca was still standing there and tried to think of something to say. She finally settled on: "The flowers looked lovely."

Bianca beamed at her. "Thanks! It all went super-well, didn't it? I think Lillian would have been so pleased. Not just because of all the compliments on the flowers, but because her basket ended up selling so well. I mean, especially considering how part of the basket was used." Bianca shivered. "Anyway, it all ended up well. I thought Lillian had gone a little crazy picking a dog basket to donate, since she didn't have pets, but it worked out really well."

Myrtle snorted. "Well, Erma Sherman put together a sports basket." They glanced at the decidedly non-athletic Erma. "I'm fairly certain Erma never played a sport in her life unless you count jump rope."

Bianca said, "I'm sure you're right. Well, I'd better run."

"Your son . . . does he have a sitter?" asked Myrtle.

"Oh, I've brought Tim here with me. He's playing on my phone in the office area. So I'm hoping the event wraps up soon so I can take him home."

Myrtle said, "I'd go ahead and start taking the floral arrangements. Then people may get the hint."

Myrtle watched thoughtfully as Bianca walked away. Bianca turned and gave Myrtle a wave, a wave that faltered slightly as she saw Myrtle's narrowed eyes.

Miles sidled up to her. "You do realize you're giving everyone death glares."

"Am I? I was just thinking," said Myrtle absently.

"Well, your thinking process looks decidedly hostile." He looked closer at her. "What on earth is it, Myrtle?"

"I don't know. I just have all sorts of things going through my head." She paused. "Why don't you come back with me for a while? We can work on crossword puzzles and maybe I'll figure out what's on my mind."

Miles looked glumly at his watch. "I was going to try and sleep."

"You won't be sleeping anyway! You've had ghastly insomnia for at least a week. You may as well come over."

Miles said, "Plus, I've worked the crossword puzzle in the paper today already."

"I have an entire crossword puzzle book that Red and Elaine gave me for my birthday. I'll tear out one of them for you."

"All right, I suppose so," said Miles.

"You don't have to sound so deflated, Miles. We'll have fun," said Myrtle.

Back at Myrtle's house, Miles said, "I'll take my car back home and walk over. There's no need to add to the constant speculation of Bradley, North Carolina that you and I are in some sort of torrid relationship."

"Good thinking. Erma would call everyone in town, otherwise."

While Miles was running his car home, Myrtle poured some potato chips in a bowl and put some cookies out on a plate. She poured a couple of glasses of ice water and pulled a crossword puzzle out of the large book.

As Miles was walking into the house, Myrtle's phone rang. She looked at it. "It's that Puddin. What on earth could she want?"

Puddin said, "Miz Myrtle, I need to come over. Think I lost somethin' at yer place."

"You couldn't possibly have. You weren't here long enough to lose anything and you haven't come back here, despite your promises to the contrary. Besides, you never even *arrive* with anything. You use all of my cleaning supplies and equipment."

Puddin said, "Jest the same, I think I did. My watch."

"A *watch*? You don't even try to keep track of time. You operate in your own Puddin time zone."

"Think I left it there," said Puddin stubbornly. "Ain't nowhere else."

Myrtle blew out a sigh. "All right then. I guess you can come by and look for it."

There was a pause on the other end. "You could look for it."

"I couldn't. I don't see it anywhere, which means if you did indeed leave it here, you put it in a weird place. I'm visiting with

Miles now and don't feel like combing my house for an errant watch."

Puddin blew a gusty sigh. "Guess I'll take Dusty's truck," she said resentfully.

"I guess so," said Myrtle, hanging up the phone. "That Puddin," she growled.

Miles said, "Well, I guess it really will be a party. Maybe you should put out some more chips and cookies."

"Puddin isn't having a bit of my food until she actually cleans my house. And Dusty isn't much better; he needs to mow again, just like Red was telling me. Honestly, it's a constant trial with those two. Come on, let's start in on our puzzles since our concentration will be blown to smithereens as soon as Puddin comes in."

Chapter Nineteen

They started working on the puzzles, Miles more cautiously with a pencil and Myrtle more boldly with a pen. Myrtle's brow furrowed in concentration. She wanted to finish hers before Miles did, but she was getting more and more distracted. She badly wanted to blame Puddin for this lack of focus, but she had the feeling it was related to something else.

"Miles."

"Mmm?" asked Miles, frowning at his puzzle.

"Do you remember when we first spoke with Bianca at the flower shop?"

Miles said absently, "Sure."

"Do you remember when she said she'd never been over to Lillian's house?"

"I guess. She said Lillian didn't like combining her professional and personal lives," said Miles. He tapped his pencil on the puzzle.

"Then we spoke with Carolyn at the library." Myrtle frowned up at the ceiling.

"The book she recommended is very good."

"Yes, I'm sure it is. But she also mentioned something. She said Lillian was hard on Bianca. Carolyn knew this because she lived next-door to Lillian and heard her speak to Bianca. At Lillian's house."

Miles shrugged. "So Bianca was wrong. She was sort of distracted when we spoke to her with her son being in the back room."

A chill went up Myrtle's spine. "Yes. But then she said something else to me tonight. She said she was glad Lillian's basket sold so well at the auction, despite the fact the feeder was used as a weapon."

"A surprising fact," said Miles.

"But Miles, no one *knew* the dog feeding station was the weapon. Red told you not to mention it to anybody. And neither he nor Perkins would have said a word."

Myrtle and Miles stared at each other. Miles put his pencil down.

The doorbell rang.

Myrtle sighed. "Puddin must have been lurking in the neighborhood to get here this quickly."

She opened the door a crack and saw Bianca there.

Myrtle carefully modulated her voice. "Hi, Bianca. Listen, I'm absolutely worn out after tonight. I'll catch up with you tomorrow, all right?"

"I don't think so," said Bianca in a hollow voice. She pointed a gun at Myrtle. "I'd like to come inside now."

Myrtle backed away from the door and Bianca pushed her way in. Bianca gave a startled cry as she saw Miles frozen at the table. She waved her gun at both of them. "Sit next to each other," she hissed. "And no funny business! I don't have a lot of time."

Myrtle walked over to plop down heavily next to Miles. "Is that because your son is by himself? You don't like to leave him in the house long, do you? That's why these murders happened at night, isn't it? You put your son to bed and then you run out really quickly to take someone's life. You don't even have to pay for a sitter that way, do you?"

Bianca glared at her. "This is all your fault."

Myrtle raised her eyebrows. "Is it? I think that statement shows a startling lack of imagination."

Miles muttered, "Myrtle. She has a gun."

"I'm well aware of that, Miles. It's pointed directly at us. I'm simply pointing out what happened here. I need to talk through the narrative so it makes some sort of sense." She paused. "You have to understand, Bianca, I don't ordinarily have guns held on me very often. I suppose my conversation with you tonight made you realize you'd made a mistake."

Bianca's hand shook as she trained the gun on them. "I saw you looking at me like you knew something."

"Sure. But I didn't know what I knew then. I only just figured it out."

"Yes, but you *were* figuring it out. You're not stupid," said Bianca with clear regret. "I heard you talking with Rowan. About evidence being faked."

Myrtle said, "One thing I noticed when Miles and I were visiting Martin at his house was Martin was a fidgety sort. You don't really think of serious readers as being fidgety, but maybe he also fidgeted with stuff while he read."

"Maybe you should get to the point," said Bianca, shaking a little more.

"The point is that the object Martin was playing with during our visit was a sterling silver business card case. Monogrammed. And I do remember he was gloating about his upcoming inheritance and becoming the owner of the flower shop. He was planning on going right over to the shop directly after we left."

Bianca shrugged, but her eyes were watchful.

Miles said slowly, "The way Martin was twirling that case and catching it, he probably did the same at the shop. Maybe he also laid it down while he was looking around. You had the chance to take it and use it as planted evidence at Tallulah's house."

"Tallulah must have seen you at the house. Maybe she told herself it was business-related. Maybe she only remembered seeing you later on. But it started bothering her and she decided to speak with Red about it," said Myrtle.

"How do you know that?" asked Bianca in a voice barely louder than a whisper.

"Because it was completely obvious at the funeral. Tallulah's eyes were trained on Red and she was clearly trying to find a private moment to talk with him. If it was obvious to me, it must have been obvious to you, too," said Myrtle.

Bianca shrugged. "All I know is, I went up to talk to her and she turned bright red and started stammering. Seemed like she knew something."

"And you went over to see her and killed her with the closest object to hand . . . one of her golf clubs," said Myrtle. She gave Bianca a reproving look. "It was your same modus operandi with

Lillian's death. Why *did* you go over to Lillian's that night? Did you go over expressly to murder her, or were you trying to have a conversation with her?"

"I was just trying to *reason* with her," whispered Bianca. The hand holding the gun shook. "That's all. She was talking about firing me because of something she said I messed up at a graduation party. But the flowers looked great! Everybody said so. There are no jobs here in Bradley and I can't move Tim to another town and another school. He's already had so many changes in his life already."

Miles frowned. "But killing Lillian wasn't going to keep you employed."

Bianca blinked at him. "I was just mad. She wouldn't listen to me. She *never* listened to me. I went there to reason with her and explain how much I needed the job. Lillian just laughed in my face and told me how bad I was. I saw red. That's all. And Martin had always been nice to me. As the new owner, I figured maybe I'd get a better deal."

"Then it was strange you decided to set him up for murdering his mother and Tallulah," said Myrtle coolly. "Although I suppose that was simply out of convenience since you had his business card holder he'd left at the shop. Still, it seems as though there might have been better candidates."

Bianca snapped, "Look, I don't have time for this. I have to get back to my son. It's not safe to leave him by himself."

"With a killer running around?" asked Myrtle laconically.

Miles gave her a look intended to make her hold her tongue.

Myrtle said, "You're not even thinking straight, Bianca. The gun you're holding on us doesn't even have a silencer. The police chief lives directly across the street."

"Well, I'm pretty close to the door," snarled Bianca. "Besides, I didn't see his car over there. I just need to hurry up, that's all."

She leveled the gun directly at Myrtle's chest. Myrtle and Miles looked at each other in panic.

Suddenly, the door was shoved open and Puddin appeared. "Where's my watch?" she demanded.

When she took in the scene in front of her: the white-faced Myrtle and Miles, and Bianca, who'd swung around with the gun, Puddin started screaming bloody murder.

The sound was ear-piercing. It was a wail very much like a siren on all the emergency vehicles rolled into one.

"Stop it! Stop it!" yelled Bianca.

Which was when Dusty pushed his way in past Puddin and waved his hedge trimmer threateningly at Bianca. Puddin continued screaming, the decibel level increasing as time went on.

While Bianca was distracted by the cacophony, Myrtle looked at Jack's toy ambulance, which Red still hadn't come by for. Miles, seeing the direction of her gaze, pushed it over to her with his foot. Myrtle slipped up behind Bianca (who was ducking as Dusty swung the hedge trimmer at her) and launched the toy at her head. Suddenly, the ambulance's broken siren roared back into life and wailed as loudly as Puddin had, lights flashing.

They all stared at the unconscious Bianca on the ground. Myrtle carefully picked up the gun and cleared her throat. "Perhaps now would be a good time for someone to call Red."

Chapter Twenty

Red and Perkins were there in minutes. They must have felt like they were on stage since the entire neighborhood was out on their lawns staring at Myrtle's house.

"I'll take that, Mama," said Red eyeing the gun Myrtle still clutched in her hand.

He and Perkins arrested Bianca. The deputy ushered her into the back of the police car as the neighborhood gaped at the scene.

Red walked back in briefly to tell everyone to leave the living room and go into the kitchen for a few minutes. He had to yell over the sound of the siren, which was still going off.

"Was *this* the toy you were trying to saddle me with?" he barked at Myrtle.

Myrtle said with a shrug, "The siren was broken until I hit Bianca with the ambulance."

"This toy stays at *your* house," said Red. Then he loudly said to everyone, "I'll be back in with Perkins in fifteen or twenty minutes."

Once he walked out, Miles picked up the ambulance and removed the batteries and the house was suddenly quiet although

Myrtle's ears were still ringing . . . whether from Puddin or the siren, she wasn't sure.

When Red and Perkins finally joined them, Puddin was finishing Myrtle's bottle of sherry and her pale cheeks were now a blotchy red. Dusty had found an ancient beer can Red had left at Myrtle's house ages ago. He'd poured the beer over ice, which just showed how desperately in need of it he was. Myrtle and Miles had made coffee.

Red and Perkins pulled some chairs from the living room into the kitchen and got their notebooks out.

"Now would somebody like to tell me what happened?" asked Red in a tight voice.

Puddin burst out indignantly, "Came in to get my watch I done left here. An' when I came in, that woman was holdin' a gun on your mama and Mr. Miles."

Myrtle said coldly. "I've never even *seen* you wear a watch."

"New revolution," said Puddin, glaring at her.

"*Resolution*," said Myrtle.

Red broke in, "Stop it! Tell me about Bianca."

Puddin gave him a resentful look. "Done told you. Her was pointin' a gun at your mama. Dusty came in to save us." She fluttered her eyelashes at Dusty and Dusty beamed shyly at her.

"That's not what happened at all!" said Myrtle. "Dusty charged in with a hedge trimmer that wasn't even turned on and created a distraction. I smashed Jack's ambulance on Bianca's head, thereby disabling her."

Perkins said politely, "Perhaps, Mr. Bradford, you could give us your version of what happened."

Miles looked pleased. "Yes. Well, Myrtle and I were working on crosswords from a book Red and Elaine had given her."

Now Red looked pleased his gift was being used.

Miles continued, "When the doorbell rang, Myrtle went to the door and Bianca forced her way in with a gun." He paused. "Myrtle had already figured out Bianca was the murderer."

Red's brow wrinkled. "How? How did she do that?"

Myrtle said smugly, "It all started when Wanda said anger is powerful."

Red's gaze lifted to the heavens.

Perkins prompted, "Mr. Bradford?"

Miles cleared his throat. "Like I said, Myrtle had already figured everything out. She knew about Carolyn Segers, for example."

Red frowned. "Carolyn, the librarian? How on earth does she figure into this?"

"Oh, she doesn't! Not really. But she gave Myrtle information about Bianca going to Lillian's house. And then Bianca spoke about the feeding station to Myrtle at the auction."

Red held his head as if it had started pounding.

"Anyway, those were all clues Myrtle needed to put two and two together," finished Miles with a shrug.

"Doesn't even have real booze in her house," Puddin muttered, shooting Myrtle a venomous look.

Red leaned forward in his chair toward Puddin and Puddin leaned backward. Red said, "Do you have any other information to add, Puddin? You or Dusty?"

Puddin considered this for a moment and then said reluctantly, "Nope."

Dusty shook his head.

"Then you can both leave," said Red crisply.

Puddin spluttered, "But her has my watch."

"If she does, which seems extremely unlikely, you can look for it the next time you're here to clean. Which is?" he looked at his mother.

"Tomorrow morning," said Myrtle immediately. She might as well get a cleaning out of this nonsense.

Puddin opened her mouth as if to contest this, saw Red's face and muttered sourly under her breath as she got up and headed for the front door with Dusty behind her.

"Now, let's try this again. Mama?" asked Red.

Myrtle took a deep breath and a momentary complacency at having the spotlight. "Bianca *was* angry. She was also really desperate. Lillian was planning on firing her after she said she botched an arrangement at an event. To Lillian, Bianca had done something unforgiveable and she was done with her. Lillian was a perfectionist and Bianca wasn't perfect."

Red made a face. "I guess she *was* desperate, considering she's a single mom and everything."

"Exactly. Bianca didn't see a way she'd be able to find another job in Bradley and she didn't want to move her son to another school district in another town after all the changes he'd already been through. So she went to Lillian's house to reason with her."

Perkins nodded. "And the conversation didn't go well, apparently."

"Lillian didn't listen to her. She was dismissive. And Bianca was frustrated, picked up the dog feeding station, and lunged at Lillian." She paused for effect and continued, "Bianca mentioned the fact an auction item was used as a weapon when she and I were speaking at the auction. And I knew no one knew that."

Red frowned. "You should have called me right when you found out."

Myrtle shook her head. "It didn't come together for me then. It was only when Miles and I were here in the quiet of the house that it occurred to me. It's when I also realized something else—that Carolyn Segers mentioned Bianca being at Lillian's house from time to time. And Bianca told Miles and me she'd never been to Lillian's."

Miles nodded.

"Plus, we'd seen Martin playing around with that silver business card case of his directly before he said he was going over to the flower shop to see his new business. The way he was fidgeting with it, it would have been easy for him to have left it on a counter or table in the back room. Bianca grabbed it, thinking it might be useful later. She planted it after she'd killed Tallulah," said Myrtle.

Perkins said, "Tallulah, living next door to Lillian, obviously saw Bianca at the house."

Myrtle said, "She either saw Bianca there or realized later that Bianca's car was there. Either way, it sounds like something that gradually dawned on her instead of something she realized right away. At the funeral, Tallulah was clearly trying to wait to speak privately with Red. Miles and I noticed it. And Bianca noticed it, too. She also noticed Tallulah was behaving oddly around her and put two and two together."

Perkins smiled at her. "Good detective work, Mrs. Clover."

Myrtle beamed at the praise.

Red sighed. "Well, all's well that ends well."

Myrtle said, "I do feel badly for Bianca's little boy. What will become of poor Tim?"

Perkins said in a steady voice, "I think he's going to be all right, even if he will have to change schools and move. The team contacted Bianca's mother and from what we understand, she's more than happy to take him in. Maybe she can even persuade the husband to pay child support."

"Or I can," glowered Red. It looked as if a phone call to Tim's dad was on his list of things to do.

Perkins stood up, "I don't think we need any other information, do we, Red?"

Red shook his head. "Not at this point. Mama, you should get some rest."

"I'm wide awake," said Myrtle, looking at him through narrowed eyes.

Perkins said mildly, "Perhaps working on the crosswords again would make for a relaxing activity. After the stress you've been through tonight."

Red glanced at the empty bottle of sherry. "I'd advise you to have a small drink, but it looks like someone eliminated that option."

Miles said quickly, "I have a bottle of chardonnay in my fridge. We could take the crosswords over there."

"Chardonnay and crosswords. I think that will work," said Myrtle.

And it did.

About the Author:

Elizabeth writes the Southern Quilting mysteries and Memphis Barbeque mysteries for Penguin Random House and the Myrtle Clover series for Midnight Ink and independently. She blogs at ElizabethSpannCraig.com/blog, named by Writer's Digest as one of the 101 Best Websites for Writers. Elizabeth makes her home in Matthews, North Carolina, with her husband. She's the mother of two.

Sign up for Elizabeth's free newsletter to stay updated on releases:

https://bit.ly/2xZUXqO

This and That

I love hearing from my readers. You can find me on Facebook as Elizabeth Spann Craig Author, on Twitter as elizabeth-scraig, on my website at elizabethspanncraig.com, and by email at elizabethspanncraig@gmail.com.

Thanks so much for reading my book...I appreciate it. If you enjoyed the story, would you please leave a short review on the site where you purchased it? Just a few words would be great. Not only do I feel encouraged reading them, but they also help other readers discover my books. Thank you!

Did you know my books are available in print and ebook formats? Most of the Myrtle Clover series is available in audio and some of the Southern Quilting mysteries are. Find the audiobooks here.

Please follow me on BookBub for my reading recommendations and release notifications.

I'd also like to thank some folks who helped me put this book together. Thanks to my cover designer, Karri Klawiter, for her awesome covers. Thanks to my editor, Judy Beatty for her help. Thanks to beta readers Amanda Arrieta and Dan Harris for all of their helpful suggestions and careful reading. Thanks to my ARC readers for helping to spread the word. Thanks, as always, to my family and readers.

Other Works by Elizabeth:

Myrtle Clover Series in Order (be sure to look for the Myrtle series in audio, ebook, and print):

Pretty is as Pretty Dies
Progressive Dinner Deadly
A Dyeing Shame
A Body in the Backyard
Death at a Drop-In
A Body at Book Club
Death Pays a Visit
A Body at Bunco
Murder on Opening Night
Cruising for Murder
Cooking is Murder
A Body in the Trunk
Cleaning is Murder
Edit to Death
Hushed Up
A Body in the Attic
Murder on the Ballot
Death of a Suitor (2021)

Southern Quilting Mysteries in Order:
Quilt or Innocence
Knot What it Seams
Quilt Trip
Shear Trouble
Tying the Knot
Patch of Trouble
Fall to Pieces
Rest in Pieces
On Pins and Needles
Fit to be Tied
Embroidering the Truth
Knot a Clue
Quilt-Ridden (2021)
The Village Library Mysteries in Order (Debuting 2019):
Checked Out
Overdue
Borrowed Time
Hush-Hush
Where There's a Will (2021)
Memphis Barbeque Mysteries in Order (Written as Riley Adams):
Delicious and Suspicious
Finger Lickin' Dead
Hickory Smoked Homicide
Rubbed Out
And a standalone "cozy zombie" novel: Race to Refuge, written as Liz Craig

Made in the USA
Las Vegas, NV
20 February 2022

44302747R00125